An Insecure Writer's Support Group Anthology

FREEDOM FOX PRESS
Dancing Lemur Press, L.L.C.
Pikeville, North Carolina
www.dancinglemurpress.com

Copyright 2018 by The Insecure Writer's Support
Group
Published by Freedom Fox Press
An imprint of:
Dancing Lemur Press, L.L.C., P.O. Box 383,
Pikeville, North Carolina, 27863-0383
www.dancinglemurpress.com

ISBN: 9781939844545

Cover design by C.R.W.

Library of Congress Control Number: 2018932408

The Insecure Writer's Support Group would like to thanks the judges who selected the stories for this anthology. We appreciate their time and effort!

Elizabeth S. Craig - Cozy mystery author for Penguin Random House, Midnight Ink, and independently.

Ion Newcombe - Editor and publisher of AntipodeanSF, Australia's longest running online speculative fiction magazine.

Anne Hawkins - Literary agent with John Hawkins & Associates, Inc.

Candace Havens - Editorial Director of Covet; author for Berkley, Entangled, and Harlequin; and an entertainment journalist.

Patricia (Pat) Stoltey - Crime fiction novelist for Five Star/Cengage.

Mason Canyon - Former journalist, book blogger, and owner of MC Book Tours.

Other anthologies from the Insecure Writer's
Support Group:

Mysteries of Death and Life
Can a lost hero find redemption?
Print ISBN 9781939844361
EBook ISBN 9781939844378

Parallels: Felix Was Here
Enter the realm of parallel universes!
Print ISBN 9781939844194
EBook ISBN 9781939844200

Table of Contents

A Stitch in Crime
By Gwen Gardner

Franny, the ghost of a former Victorian madam, hovered over my shoulder.

"Push the needle through from the underside, then cross diagonally and push the needle back through the material. No, dear, cross it—*cross* it. That's why it's called *cross*-stitch."

"No need to get cross about it," I joked. "Ow!" A bright-red bubble sprang up on my thumb where I had jammed the needle into it.

"You didn't warn me this was going to be a dangerous activity." After my last haunting case turned into murder, I wanted a nice, safe, boring hobby. Cross-stitch sounded like a good idea at the time.

"Oh, do be careful, dear," Franny said, with her usual *tsk.*

For the record, I am *not* clumsy. Spirits tend to be needy, and meeting strange ghosts can get dicey. When things get dicey, stuff happens. *That's all.*

I encounter a lot of ghosties in Sabrina Shores, a medieval market town boasting eight hundred years of history. Where there's history, ghosts reside. In my opinion, we had the highest ghost population per capita in all of England. A ghost magnet like me ought to know.

I held the embroidered cloth up for Franny's inspection, but even I could see gaps where I'd missed stitches—and still others where the stitches resembled the Leaning Tower of Pisa instead of the Statue of Liberty. It looked like a six-year-old stitched it. *Almost.*

Franny eyed my work and blinked several times. Teaching me to embroider was not her best idea ever. To her credit though, she rearranged her features into a smile and went with it. "Yes, that's it, dear. You're getting the hang of it."

Today Franny wore a periwinkle-blue dress with black lace trim, cinched at the waist to within an inch of her afterlife. Thank goodness she didn't need to breathe. The dress complemented her indigo-blue eyes, and her shining black hair twisted into an up-do that reflected true Victorian artistry.

Related somewhere up the meandering family vine, we were almost mirror images of each other— except she got the full stack to fill out her bustier, and I got shafted. The unfairness rankled, but push-up bras and padding worked wonders. Where Franny rocked a stylish wardrobe, I preferred a more relaxed fit: tie-dyed leggings and sweat shirt, my unbrushed hair wadded into a topknot. My relaxed style proved to be the bane of Franny's existence. If I had a pound for every time she lamented, "How will you ever catch a man wearing that?" or "You're not wearing that, are you?" I'd be a rich woman today.

Far from being rich, I ate ramen noodles too often for comfort. That would change when I landed a job—a real job, not the ghostbusting kind.

A sharp rap at the door pierced the room. I locked glances with Franny, then checked the clock over the fireplace. "It's after ten; who could be stopping by now?" I laid my cross-stitch aside and padded to the front door. I peeked through the peephole. My hunky ex-boyfriend's distorted face peered back.

"It's Badger." I glanced down at my comfy clothes with a twinge of regret. Maybe Franny had a point.

Franny's jaw dropped open, and she flapped her hands. "And look at the state of you! Quick now, go change. Brush your hair. You look like a carpetbag lady."

I shook my head. Franny's mastery of modern vernacular needed help on occasion. "You mean bag lady." I ignored her advice and shot back the deadbolt. "Badger, this is a surprise!"

"Sorry it's so late, but I come bearing gifts." He produced a bag from Java Jane's and a cardboard holder containing two coffees. "Italian roast, extra large, extra shot, extra strong."

He knew me well. I snatched the bag. "In that case, you should come in."

Badger trailed me to the kitchen. Shrugging off his jacket, he shivered and glanced around. "Hi, Franny." Badger knew about the cold spots in my flat and why they were there. He knew about Franny but couldn't hear her. Thank goodness for small favors. If he could hear half of what she said...

"Good evening, lover boy." Franny sidled up to him and ran a seductive finger along his cheek, then trailed down his arm. She air-smooched his cheek, and he shivered again.

"Franny says hello." I shot her a pointed look. "She was just leaving."

She glared at me. "I never get to have any fun."

I snorted. Franny's afterlife included a parade of adoring men and countless parties. My life consisted of learning how to cross-stitch from a ghost of questionable morals on a Friday night. And that only because she pitied my nonexistent social life. Her quest to find me a man proved relentless. And annoying. I could find a man if I wanted. I still had moves up my sleeve.

I pushed up my sleeves and tore into the bag. A variety of pastries nestled inside, beckoning, like a treasure chest full of jewels. "Bagels, croissants, snickerdoodles, macaroons..." I looked up and met Badger's eyes. "Okay, spill the coffee beans. This is serious indeed." I twisted the bag top into a tight taper and pushed it away, then sat back and crossed my arms. "You're not here on a Friday night for my titillating company."

"You wound me." He splayed his hand over his heart as if I'd punctured it with an arrow.

"Yeah, yeah. Come on, you brought all my favorite junk foods, so out with it."

He sighed. "You're right. This isn't exactly a social call."

He didn't meet my eyes or answer right away. Instead he crossed to the cupboard and pulled out a plate, then made a big production of untwisting and smoothing out the mangled bag. Pastries were arranged to their best advantage. "As it happens, I have a friend in need."

"Uh-huh." I snatched a macaroon and bit it in half. The sweet and chewy coconut seduced my taste buds. I shoved the rest in my mouth and continued. "Let me guess. This friend of yours has a mischievous ghost who's creating havoc and making life miserable."

"In a word, yes."

I sighed. "I'm not a ghostbuster. I need a real job." I'd applied for numerous positions with no response. I dreamed of eating real food instead of ramen noodles every night.

"I know." He plucked a blueberry scone from the pile and broke it in half. "But it's a paying gig, and let's face it: you need money."

Someone had a big mouth. Probably me. "How much?" I may not like dealing with spirits, but I could be bought for the right price. Like a steak-and-potato dinner, perhaps with a nice bottle of Cabernet thrown in.

"The going rate," Badger said. He shoved half the scone in his mouth and chewed while I waited. "A thousand pounds."

The macaroon lodged in my throat, trapping coconut-coffee juice at the back of my nasal passages. I managed to swallow the lump before anything shot from my nose, but a coughing fit ensued. Once that subsided, I wiped my watery eyes on the back on my hand. "When do I start?" I choked out.

"Don't you want to know what it is first?"

"I'd exorcise the devil himself for a thousand pounds," I said, then hesitated. "It's not the devil himself...is it?"

He laughed and shook his head. "No, lucky for you. It sounds tame. A friend of mine owns the Candy Cupboard. A few days ago she came in to find candy scattered all over the floor. Her assistant swore she swept and mopped before closing. So she checked the security cameras."

"And caught the culprit red-handed?" I prompted.

"Not exactly. A bin opened by itself. The candy scoop rose into the air, as if someone lifted it up, then dumped it onto the floor. At six o'clock every night since, the scenario repeats itself."

I shook my head. "A wanton waste of candy, a true crime indeed." Or more like a mischievous ghost with a sweet tooth.

"True, it's only a handful of candy at a time..." he said.

"Uh oh. I feel a 'but' coming," I said.

"Apparently the spirit has an attack of conscience, and attempts to pick up and put the candy back," he said.

"Sounds like a good plan to me. I wonder if this ghostie is for hire?" I joked. "Better yet, I wonder if Franny can be trained."

"I heard that, you ungrateful scamp," Franny called through the ether.

I ignored her.

Badger continued. "The problem is health and

11

safety standards. The whole bin has to be chucked."

"Ah. Loss of inventory can be costly," I agreed.

"And then there's the small matter of scaring the customers," he added.

I snorted. "A little flying candy? I've seen worse." I sent up a silent prayer that our sweet-toothed ghostie didn't have a toothache by the time I got there.

* * *

I arranged to meet Maisy, the candy-store owner, at closing time on Saturday night. Leaving my flat, I wound through a series of narrow cobblestoned passages to the town center. Half-timbered Elizabethan and Tudor architecture lined the square, a picture-perfect backdrop for a Dickensian Christmas scene. A towering Christmas tree, dusted with snow earlier in the day, lit up the square. Bright lights blinked, lighting up the red and gold bulbs hanging from the branches. "Jingle Bell Rock" filtered through outdoor speakers so shoppers could enjoy the music.

Silver swirls of fog rolled in off the nearby Sabrina River and long, misty fingertips pinched exposed cheeks and noses. Rather than dampen holiday spirits, it seemed to spread goodwill and cheer, as if touched by the calming torch of the Ghost of Christmas Present.

But as I wove through the milling crowds, I avoided all eye contact with any specter resembling the ghosts of Christmas past, present, or future—I could only take on one haunting gig at a time—and continued on to the candy store.

The window display at the Candy Cupboard stopped me in my tracks. A Santa's village made of gingerbread houses with gumdrop chimneys, candy-floss snow, and chocolate reindeer encompassed the entire window.

Franny popped in beside me. "Every child's dream, isn't it?" A wistful note entered her voice. She'd never had children. I often thought that was why she'd attached herself to me.

A bell chimed over the door when I entered, but no one came to greet me. Glancing around, I saw that the Candy Cupboard was a popular place. The air prickled with otherworld energy. I wandered the shop, wanting to get a feel for the place before I met Maisy.

The store was long and narrow. Three rows of clear-lidded plastic bins, broken up only by a kiosk in the center of the store, held every kind of candy imaginable, from Airheads to gummy bears to licorice sticks and gobstoppers. The kiosk contained the candies made on site. Each filling station provided scoops and cute plastic bags decorated with candy canes in which to stuff candy and pay by weight.

I continued down another aisle and noticed the drop in temperature as I walked. A swoosh of cold air blasted toward me, followed by the spirit of an older woman zipping through a candy bin to hover inside my personal space. I sucked in a breath at the unexpected cold front, then exhaled a plume of condensation.

I managed to keep my cool. "Hello," I said through frozen lips. "I'm Indigo Eady."

Instead of responding in kind, she narrowed her eyes and shook a finger in my face. "I'm watching you. My granddaughter loses a lot of merchandise to theft."

The accusation stung. I'd given her no reason to suspect me of stealing. Unless you counted prowling the aisles while casting covert glances over my shoulder like a sneaky thief.

Maybe she had a point.

Franny jammed her hands on her hips. "Of all the nerve. Miss Eady would never steal. In fact, she's here to help."

The elderly spirit, her steel-gray hair tightly

permed against her head, wore a purple polyester pantsuit with Velcro-strapped trainers. She cocked her head toward Franny, a malicious gleam in her eyes. "And who are you, her grandmother?"

Oh no, she did not just go there.

"Why you insufferable old cow—" Franny began.

"Hello, can I help you?" Footsteps approached from behind, and I turned to see a somewhat plump young blond woman trod toward me. She wore a white smock, and her name tag read, "Maisy Potter, Master Confectioner."

I smiled and stuck out my hand. "I'm Indigo Eady. Badger Bagley sent me to help with your, erm, security problem."

She hesitated—I suppose she expected someone sporting a white zip-up onesie and a portable hoover strapped to her back—but seconds later reached for my hand with both of hers and shook with such vigor that my teeth rattled. I extracted my hand before any serious damage occurred to my dental work.

"I'm Maisy," she said. "I am so happy you're here, Indigo; I'm at my wit's end. I mentioned to Badger what happened, and he didn't think I was daft at all. I can tell you, I was happy he believed me. I mean, it's crazy, isn't it? Ghosts aren't real."

I didn't have a chance to respond.

Maisy continued without taking a breath, as if she had to get it all out at once. "And then when he said he knew someone who could help..." Tears sprang to her eyes. "It is so good of you to come."

"I'm happy to help, Maisy," I told her. "Don't worry, we'll figure this out. Is there somewhere we can talk for a few minutes?"

"Of course. My office is in back." She led us toward the gingerbread house construction area, circled around, then stopped at a door in the rear.

"Be sure to ask about the money," Franny said,

zipping along behind us. "You'll need a contract, nice and legal-like."

"That's right," the grandmother ghost sniped, "it's always about the money."

"You can throw this old harpy into the exorcism for free," Franny said to my backside.

"I'm not going anywhere," the spirit said. "You can't make me."

I sighed. We hadn't gotten off to a good start with the resident ghost.

Maisy unlocked her office door and flipped the light switch. I stepped inside, then turned and hissed, "Wait here!" before closing the door on the pair of them. I could still hear them having a go at each other on the other side of the door.

"Tell me about what's been happening," I said, taking the chair she offered. "When did it start?"

"Last Tuesday night, right before closing," Maisy said. "It frightened the children horribly. I had to do some quick thinking to reassure them it was part of the scene left over from Halloween. I've caught it on camera. Let me show you."

I circled her desk to peer over her shoulder as she worked to bring up the security footage on the computer screen. "Here it is," Maisy said, sitting back.

We watched the scoop lift candy from the bin and dump it on the floor. Seconds later, a few pieces floated back into the bin on their own. Childish voices screamed in the background.

Maisy looked up at me. "Badger says you know how to handle this sort of thing. Can you stop it?"

"Yes, I'm sure I can." Except I wasn't at all sure.

"The sooner the better," Maisy said, pulling out a checkbook from her desk drawer. "I have to dispose of all the candy from the bin every time it happens. I can't sell candy that's been on the floor, and there is no way of separating the clean candy from the other.

I don't want my shop to have a haunted reputation either. That only works at Halloween." She scribbled something across the check and handed it over. "Badger said to pay you half now and the other half when it's taken care of. Is that right?"

Bless him. "Yes, thank you." I glanced at the check for £500 then tucked it into my pocket before she changed her mind. A case of nerves took hold. What if I couldn't stop the haunting? There is no magic formula. I'd solved a couple of murders in the past, but mostly I stumbled around until I came across the answer, and nearly always after putting myself in mortal danger.

Still, if a ghost haunted a particular spot, there had to be a reason. I only had to find that reason, fix the problem, then cross the ghost over. Easy peasy, right?

Franny poked her head through the door. "Indigo, come quick. There's something you should see."

I glanced at Maisy as I rose from my seat. "Uh, I just, uh, need to..."

"Of course, you need to see the spot, don't you?" she began, hot on my heels. I stopped next to Franny alongside a row of candy bins.

Franny pointed at a spot on the floor. The shape of a crumpled body lay etched into the linoleum like a crime-scene chalk outline.

Maisy stopped short and grasped my arm. "What is that? How'd it get there?"

"It's a death spot," I explained. "Sometimes with a traumatic death, the spirit is attached to the spot where they died."

"But they usually disappear a few days after death," Franny added, although Maisy couldn't hear her. She floated around the outline to take in another view.

"Have you lost anyone recently?" I asked Maisy.

"Any deaths occur here? Anniversary of a death, or…?"

"My grandmother passed away last October. She used to help out here." Maisy smiled then. "Her name was Hermione Potter. The children got a kick out of it, you know, because of the *Harry Potter* books." Her gaze searched the room as if she might spot her grandmother. "You don't think it's my grandmother, do you? I hate the thought that she might not be at rest."

"Did she pass here?" I asked, dodging the question. Getting the cranky old woman to cross over could be potentially problematic. Old Mrs. Potter appeared to be quite attached to her granddaughter.

"She died at home," Maisy said, her eyes widening and close to panic.

"Then it couldn't be hers," I said, glancing at Mrs. Potter. "I'm sure your grandmother is at peace." I'd have to work on her after I solved the current mystery surrounding the death spot. But if it wasn't Grandma Potter's death spot, then who did it belong to?

Maisy's fingers shook as she slid a key off her keychain and handed it to me. "You'll want to stay on after we leave. Be careful, won't you?"

"No worries. Leave it to me."

Once Maisy departed, I contemplated the death spot. "Why would a death spot show up now if no one died here recently?" I asked Franny.

"I wish I knew," Franny said.

"Whatever happened on Tuesday at six o'clock started the ball rolling." I glanced up and caught a shadow cross the end of the aisle.

Mrs. Potter floated up next to me. "It's another child out to steal the candy. You won't catch that one though. She's a slippery character."

"What do you know about it?" Franny asked.

"More than you lot. A girl showed up here about

a week ago to raid the candy bins. Makes a go at it every night now, regular, like clockwork."

A sneeze burst from the ether. "Bless you," I said to Mrs. Potter automatically.

"That wasn't me. I'm healthy as a horse," the elderly ghost said, crossing her arms over her chest. Her gaze challenged me to contradict her.

Healthy as a horse she may be, but dead all the same.

Lights flickered overhead. I stood rooted, not out of fear—well, not much—but because I didn't want to scare the child's spirit off until I could figure out what she wanted.

A golden glow hovered at the end of the aisle and formed into the shape of a little girl. She wore a knee-length, beige-brown plaid dress, and a blue jumper buttoned all the way to her throat. A scarf folded into a triangle shape covered her head, the ends knotted under her chin. Her nose was pink and runny.

She floated toward me and stopped before a candy bin halfway up the aisle. The lid creaked open. She dug the scoop deep inside and pulled it out, brimming with yellow lemon drops.

I took a deep breath, prepared to approach the girl. Before I could, the spirit of an older man, pear shaped with wispy hair, appeared. "You there! What are you doing? Drop that!"

The girl jumped. Lemon drops scattered and bounced across the floor. She bent and grasped at bouncing candies and tossed them toward the bin. Her hands shook, her efforts awkward. A wail rent the air.

The hair stood up on my nape.

The girl fell to the floor and laid still, her little form filling the death spot like a glove.

"Stop that! Can't you see she's scared?" I scolded the man. I ran forward and dropped down next to the girl. My heart ached for her. To reenact her death over and over was heart-wrenching.

To give him credit, the pudgy man looked shocked. "I—I didn't know—I didn't think," he sputtered.

"The poor dear only wanted a bit of candy," Franny said, stooping to stroke the girl's forehead.

The man's cheeks puffed out. "But this is medicine. It requires a prescription from a licensed physician. I can't have every customer helping themselves. It just isn't done." He stared at the girl lying sprawled on the floor. "Still an' all, I wish I hadn't yelled at the poor waif."

Wait, what? "Medicine? But...this is candy," I said.

"In our realm it's candy," Mrs. Potter said, as if she was still alive. "But this was Mr. Bloombury's Chemist Dispensary long before my granddaughter opened a candy shop."

"So the girl wasn't after candy," Franny said, "but what...cough drops?"

The old guy scratched his head. "What are you talking about?"

"It's not your chemist shop anymore, Mr. Bloombury. This is a sweet shop now," Mrs. Potter said, shaking her head. "I tell him every day, but he forgets."

A tiny sneeze turned all our heads back to the girl.

"Now, now, dear. Let Aunt Franny help you." The girl sat up, wiping her nose on the inside of a frayed sleeve.

"Well, I'll be," Mrs. Potter said. "I've been trying for days to catch her. She escaped every time I tried."

I shot warning daggers at the old woman. "We did not catch her. She's free to go if she wants. But we'd like to help her if we can."

Mrs. Potter huffed but remained silent.

19

"What's your name, dear?" Franny asked the little spirit girl.

"Beatrix. Beatrix Hamilton, miss," the girl said through nasally passages.

"That's a lovely name." I sat cross-legged next to her. "I'm Indigo."

"How can we help you, dear?" Franny asked.

The girl's eyes darted to the chemist, then back to Franny. "I need medicine for the sister, miss. She's awful sick. Coughing up a lungful, miss." Beatrix sneezed again. "Can you 'elp me?"

The chemist cleared his throat. "Well of course we will. Now that I know what you want."

"We'll try our best, Beatrix. Who is the sister? Do you know where I can find her?" I asked.

"Sister Rose is at Saint Nicholas."

"Can you show me?" I asked.

Tears sprang to her eyes, and she dashed them away. She shook her head. "I can't leave. I tried and tried, miss. Only I keep dying"—her gaze shot to the death spot but didn't linger—"right there," she finished in a whisper.

* * *

"Do we knock or just go in?" I glanced up at the wooden sign hanging askew, the paint faded and peeling. Saint Nicholas's Church and Home for Children had seen better days.

Franny quirked a brow. "You're asking me? I'm not at all sure I can cross the threshold safely, given the moral ambiguity of my former profession. I haven't seen the inside of a church in a hundred and fifty years."

"From what I remember, churches are always open." I clutched the handle, turned, and pushed. Nothing. I wiggled the handle, then shoved harder. "It's locked." I knocked on the door and waited. No one came.

"I'll have a look, shall I?" Franny hiked her skirts to her knees and poked one leg through the door, as if testing the temperature of water in a swimming pool. She pulled her leg back out, wiggling her foot, still attached and in good working order. She smiled. "That answers that question!" She dropped her skirts and floated through the door.

I scanned the area and waited for her to return. Frost-bitten grass lay dormant in the early-morning gray. The cemetery beyond was blanketed with dead leaves, which stirred in the breeze. Twigs reached through in spots like hand bones clawing up through the grave.

Seconds later, Franny zipped back through the door. "There's a bell inside next to the door"—she pointed to the overgrown area next to the door jamb covered with dead vines and spider webs—"try the pull rope."

I dug through the vines and found the bell pull and gave it a tug. The peal resounded loud enough to wake the dead, but it did the trick.

A tiny window in the door opened. A pair of brown eyes peered out from a wrinkled face, a black-and-white nun's habit just visible in the frame. "Yes, can I help you?" an elderly woman's voice asked.

I smiled. "I'm Indigo Eady. I've come to see if I might speak to Sister Rose?"

"I'm sorry, Miss Eady. We don't have anyone here by that name."

"Oh." My heart sank. What if Sister Rose had died? Beatrix's style of dress was mid-twentieth century, maybe 1950s. Sixty years was a long time. Sister Rose could be long gone.

"I'm Sister Lydia. What is this about?" the nun asked.

I held up the plastic bag with the cough drops that Beatrix insisted would save Sister Rose. "Just delivering these for a friend."

"This is a private facility now. It has been for the past twenty years," Sister Lydia said. "I've been here for years. We have never had a sister named Rose who I can remember."

"Would you have records that might tell me where Sister Rose went?" I asked.

"No. I'm sorry," she said.

Before I could ask anything else, the peephole clicked shut with finality.

"Well, she was certainly in a hurry," Franny said. She turned to me. "Now what?"

"I have to find Sister Rose, and Saint Nicholas's is our only lead. The answer is here. We need to get inside." I stepped back from the door. Looking to the right, I spied a muddy path that led around the building. "This way."

I ignored the mud sucking at my boots. Franny tiptoed behind me, lifting her skirts as if she might get the hems dirty.

We rounded the back of the building, then turned and trod down a short flight of stairs that led belowground. Kitchens in Victorian times were always on a lower level. Saint Nicholas might be a private facility now, but I'd be willing to bet they still had kitchen staff. I rapped on the door. A middle-aged woman with her hair pinned in a bun and wearing a knee-length, faded orange dress answered the door, wiping her hands on a stained apron.

"Good morning. I knocked at the front door, but..." I let the sentence trail off.

"Oh, do come in. I can't hear the bell ring from back here. I'm Mrs. Cathstone. I do a bit of cooking and cleaning for the sisters," she said. "I'm about to have a cuppa; would you like to join me?" Mrs. Cathstone asked, moving over to the table where a teapot wrapped in a cozy stood next to a plate of chocolate biscuits.

With regret, I held up the bag of lemon "cough" drops. "Thank you, but I came to deliver these to..."

"Ah, those will be for Sister Judy," she said with a *tsk*. "She's been under the weather."

I nodded and hoped the good Lord would forgive the subterfuge.

"Through that door, the staircase to the left, last door on the right," she said.

I thanked her and pushed through the door and rounded the corner.

"Well played. You could have been an actress on the stage," Franny said, keeping pace beside me. "Have I told you about my time in the theater?"

Only a million times.

* * *

Photographs of children lined the walls. Girls of all ages, and although their manner of dress was plain and their clothing worn, they wore smiles and hammed it up for the camera. These girls were loved and happy.

A short way down the corridor, Franny stopped and peered closely at a black and white photograph, the edges yellowed and curling with age. "Indigo, look here. This looks like Beatrix." A blond girl in pigtails with pink ribbons sat on a blanket full of picnic foods. The sun shone behind her, and a river could be seen in the background. The girl smiled big for the camera.

"Yes, it definitely is Beatrix," I said. "Come on, we need to find where they keep the records before we get caught and thrown out."

We split up to search for a records room. From what I could tell, only two other nuns now inhabited the private facility, along with Sister Lydia. I'd searched three rooms already, but found nothing. I'd just managed to avoid running into Sister Lydia only moments before by ducking into the last room on the corridor.

Franny floated through the door behind me. "Have you found anything?"

"Not yet," I said. "That woman is everywhere, I tell you."

"You must have met Sister Lydia," a feeble voice behind me said. I turned to find an old woman lying in a bed, her silvery head propped up on a pile of pillows. Her cheeks were pale, her blue eyes rheumy. We were alone in the room.

"Oh! I'm sorry, I didn't know, I didn't mean..." I began, at a loss for words.

She smiled sweetly. "I've spent a fair amount of time losing the sister myself. Sister Lydia means well, but she can be a bit..."

"Overbearing?" Franny added, sauntering around the room, still searching for records.

The old woman glanced at Franny. "Yes."

Franny's eyes widened. I don't think any other living person had ever acknowledged her before. The old woman smiled. "My death must be close if I can see spirits in my room."

"I am so sorry, Sister. We didn't mean to intrude on your passing," I blurted without thinking. "I mean, not that I know..."

"How is it that you can see her too?" the old woman asked, glancing again at Franny.

"It's a gift"—I glanced at Franny—"mostly."

"Ha-ha," Franny said, shaking her head. She drifted over to the woman's bed. "Pay her no mind. She does plenty of good with her gift...when she wants to. I'm Franny Bishop. I'm pleased to make your acquaintance." She nodded her head once politely.

"Well, this is a turn of events," the old woman said. "The most excitement I've had in days. I'm Sister Judith. They say my heart is giving out. I'm eighty-five years old, you know. I've had a long life." She closed her eyes briefly, and I worried we were overtiring her.

"Perhaps we should go," I said.

"No, don't go," Sister Judith said. "I like young people around me. We don't get many since the orphanage closed."

Franny drifted over to look at the far wall, which was plastered with children's artwork. There must have been hundreds. Crayon drawings, finger paintings, pencil, and markers. "Indigo, I think you should see this," Franny said.

"What is it?" I sauntered over to join her. In the center of the wall hung a cross-stitch pendant of an angel mounted inside a picture frame. Stitched in childish lettering at the bottom were the words "Sister Rose."

A tingle crept up my spine. I turned to the old nun lying in the bed. "This cross-stitch. It says 'Sister Rose.' Do you know Sister Rose?"

She raised a weak, shaking finger and pointed to a corkboard nailed to the wall. Hundreds of photos were pinned to it. "The photo in the middle. That's Sister Rose. Once upon a time, a lifetime ago, I knew her very well indeed." The old nun closed her eyes, her breathing ragged.

"Do you know where I can find her?" I asked.

The nun opened her eyes. "I wasn't always Sister Judith. I grew up as Rosalie Randall. I served as Sister Rose as a novitiate right here at Saint Nicholas. When I took my vows, my name was changed to Judith."

"Do you know a child named Beatrix Hamilton?" I asked her.

Her eyes saddened. "Beatrix was such a lovely child. One of the first children I cared for when I came here. We had a special bond." Her eyes grew wary. "Why do you ask?"

"Because Beatrix has been trying to get a gift to you." I pulled the bag of lemon drops from my handbag.

"I don't understand," Sister Judith said. "Beatrix has been dead for over sixty years."

I went on to explain the haunting that began on Tuesday night at the Candy Cupboard and how I'd been hired to stop it, then about meeting Beatrix and promising that we'd help find Sister Rose and get her the "medicine" she needed.

The nun's eyes watered. "I became ill on Tuesday evening." She gazed into the distance, as if remembering. "Back in 1950, a horrible flu went around. So many of us came down with it. I was very ill, close to death, they say. Beatrix had gone to bed. Nobody knew how ill she really was. The next morning she wasn't in her bed or the breakfast room. We couldn't find her anywhere." Sister Judith was silent for a few minutes. "Then a policeman came. Beatrix had been found dead at Bloombury's Dispensary. Somehow she'd gotten locked in after hours. Nobody knew she was there, or why. We could only speculate."

"She wanted to get medicine for you," I said softly.

Franny looked thoughtful. "I think that Sister Judith being so close to dying again must have been the trigger for little Beatrix to come back and try once more."

"That's right," I agreed. "Where she failed before, she had another chance to get it right." I opened the bag and plucked out a piece of candy. "They're lemon drops. I hope you like them."

She smiled and took it from me. "They're my favorite."

* * *

Franny glanced up from her embroidery. "Someone's here."

"How do you..." I began, before a hollow-sounding knock echoed into the room. "Never mind." I laid my cross-stitch aside and padded to the door. "If Badger thinks he can show up here at this hour..." I swung the door open.

Beatrix hovered at the door. Sister Rose shimmered beside her, a familiar decorative plastic bag clutched in her hand. Sister Rose appeared as she had in the aged photo pinned to her corkboard. A young woman about to take holy orders. She wore a simple white veil, matching dress with black tights, and sensible black shoes.

"Hello, miss." Beatrix bobbed a curtsy and smiled wide. "I've come to thank you proper-like for 'elping Sister Rose and me."

As soon as I'd found Sister Rose and had given her the lemon drop "cough drops," the candy store haunting had stopped. Sister Rose had passed not long after my visit.

"We both wanted to stop and thank you before we move on," Sister Rose added. "You and Miss Bishop performed a great service in helping us to reunite."

"I'm so glad we could help." I couldn't help smiling seeing the two of them together. They'd waited a long time.

"Good-bye..." Sister Rose faded away, Beatrix's hand clasped tightly in hers.

I closed the door and heaved a sigh. "You know, sometimes this ability I have to speak with spirits can be a burden. So often they want something from me and I feel completely helpless. But at times like this, it feels like a privilege that I could help."

"You did more than help," Franny said. "Without you, they would never have found each other again."

"I couldn't have done it without you," I said. "You spotted the cross-stitch angel of Sister Rose. So it was you who really found her."

A pink tinge rose to her cheeks, the closest thing to a blush I'd even seen on Franny.

"Little Beatrix waited sixty years to find a way to

help Sister Rose. What a lovely bond they shared. A bit like us, don't you think?" Franny glanced up from under her lashes, as if to gauge my reaction.

I smiled. "Yes. Exactly like us."

The End

Gwen Gardner writes sweet, cozy mysteries with a few ghosts thrown in to stir things up. Since ghosts feature prominently in her stories, she has a secret desire to meet one face to face—but will run screaming for the hills if she ever does. Gwen adores adventure, travel and anything chocolate.
www.gwengardner.blogspot.com
www.gwengardner.com
www.twitter.com/LadyGwenTweets
www.facebook.com/IndigoEady

Gussy Saint and the Case of the Missing Co-ed
By C.D. Gallant-King

I *watched the fist coming toward my face with a vague fascination, as one might observe a butterfly that has landed on his knee or a scientist examining some particularly thrilling bacteria in a Petri dish. I counted every wrinkle and groove on the rough skin of the hand, noticed a distinct scar across the second and third knuckles—the result of a previous fight or perhaps a can-opener accident. Behind the fist I saw the old clock on the wall "tick" off a single second. The clock was one of those big, round deals with the black arms that looked like it should be hanging in a doctor's office. Actually, I knew for a fact that it once hung in a doctor's office, because that's where I'd stolen it.*

My eyes on the time—quarter-past-nine—I flashed back to all the other times I was punched in the face.

Bernie Stapleton in Grade 2.

My dad.

Rick Goodwin in Grade 4.

Sally Simpson in Grade 7.

My dad again.

Sally Simpson's boyfriend in Grade 8.

My da—this was going to take awhile, and I wasn't even up to my actual fighting career.

* * *

As I awaited the inevitable impact, my mind wandered back to the day this investigation went downhill like a screaming hippo in a bobsled. The moment when I seriously started reconsidering my decision to be a private dick.

Rain fell in Mount Vernon. It always rained in

Mount Vernon. The rest of the country was suffering through sub-arctic temperatures and enough snow to make an Inuit pack up his dogsled and move south for the winter, but if you looked out the window in Mount Vernon you'd swear Noah was going to buzz by on a jet ski any moment.

The rain was cold and chewed down deep into your bones like a junkie trying to bite through a baggie of heroin. I hated a rain like that. It always portended something terrible on the horizon, like spilling a baggie of heroin all over the toilet of a bus station restroom.

It was a place I'd found myself more than once that I hoped not to visit again.

I was a long way from that bus station restroom and the lifestyle that had driven me to the stoniest of rock bottoms. In many ways, you can't get away from that place—not completely—but I made improvements. I had steered clear of hard drugs and bus stations for nearly six years, though I replaced that addiction with liquor, gambling, and women.

I was sitting in my office, which was only slightly less filthy than the aforementioned restroom, with my shiny wing tips up on the desk and my chair tilted back to the point of toppling, lost in my thoughts around the biggest case of my life. I heard my new secretary's heels clicking across the tile in the outer office and it snapped me back to reality so fast I nearly ended up on the floor. That woman was probably the biggest score of my life, and I hadn't even slept with her yet.

I found her in a club downtown, drunk out of her mind and looking for a fight and a lay, and not necessarily in that order. Usually that's just the way I like my lady friends, but before I could move in another broad knocked over her drink and sparked off the most beautiful cat fight I'd ever seen. I'll dream about those two gorgeous women rolling around on the floor, tearing at each other, until the day I die.

It had taken all my pull and connections down at the precinct to get her off. By that I mean I had to get the police captain off—twice—which was a moderate challenge but not really much of a hardship. The girl was so happy not be going to jail or deported that she threw herself at my offer of a job. And of course, by that I mean I had to beg and plead with her to work for me and had to offer way more money than I can afford. It was worth it, though. It was a little piece of heaven to have a nice pair of legs around the office, and the new bird had legs to die for.

She called herself George. I had no idea if that was her real name, and frankly I didn't give a damn. With legs like that she could call herself whatever she wanted.

She was blonde, brazen, and British. I would love to say she was bouncy as well, but she wasn't—she was cut from granite, with a wit and an icy grey stare that could slice through a man as quick and easy as a prison shiv but only half as merciful.

But those legs, oh those legs. A man would give up his last dime and skip his last meal on the way to the chair for a chance to see just how far those gams went up that black pencil skirt. I couldn't help but watch them slink and sway as she crossed the floor, her heels clicking on the tile like tiny gunshots in my head. She came right up to my open door and leaned against the frame with a quizzical look on her face. She might have just been wondering if she left the iron on this morning, but I liked to think she was wondering what it felt like to be curled up in my arms with no pants between us.

"Who are you speaking to?" She tilted her head to the side like a puppy wondering where her next treat was coming from.

"What do you mean?"

Her lips twisted. "Did you just call me a dog?"

Just like I said, the girl was brazen. "You, honey? Not a chance. But you if you want me to put you on a leash and parade you around—"

"You are narrating yourself again, aren't you?" She glared at me incredulously.

"What?"

"There! You just did it again! You said I glared 'incredulously.' I don't think you even you used the word properly."

I sat back in my chair, more shocked than if she had slapped me. "How did you know?"

"Because you talk to yourself *all the time*. At first I thought you were just leaving the telly on. Then it got a bit creepy. Then kinda cute. Now you're just annoying to no end. You *are* getting better, though. I can barely hear you anymore, but I can still see your lips moving."

This was an interesting development. Did that mean she heard me when I was daydreaming about undressing her and—

"Stop it! Look, it was wonderful of you to give me a job—my work visa was about to expire and with Henry going to jail, they probably would have shipped me back home. I don't even want to know how you got the police to drop the charges. But just because I appreciate the job doesn't mean I have to put up with your insane...whatever it is you're doing."

George stood with her hands on her hips and a fierce look on her face like— *Ahem* "Sorry. You're welcome?"

"How many of those Mickey Spillane novels did you read while you were sleeping on that bus station bench?"

"Someone left a whole box of them in the john. A few of them were soggy, but the man's a damn fine writer."

She rolled her eyes. "Anyway, your one o'clock is here."

"I have an appointment?"

"Yes, I made it for you this morning. It's in your computer."

"I have a computer?"

"It's a good thing you hired me as your secretary. You are completely helpless."

I liked a girl with a good head to go with a good set of— "Sorry. I can't help myself. By all means. Send them in."

George looked as good walking away as she did coming toward you. The girl swayed like a cobra, and was nearly as deadly—

"I can still hear you!"

Poor broad. She was lost without her man. That Henry bloke, he had been her meal ticket, keeping her in all the luxury that a goddess like her deserved. But the problem with placing your well-being into the hands of a crook like Henry Nutter is eventually the law is going to catch up with him, and you're going to find yourself out on your shapely ass. A lady like George, she deserved better than that.

There also existed the small issue that I was the one responsible for Nutter getting locked up. While that was completely coincidental, I kept my fingers crossed that George didn't find out about it.

Nutter worked for the man they called The Duke of Mount Vernon, the head of the British crime family that controlled the seedy underside of our cold, wet Washington city. Don't ask me why a bunch of stuck-up English criminals were rolling in a tenth-rate American town. Eccentric, I guess. They controlled drugs and prostitution all through the North West, and they were the kingpins of a vast underground fighting and gambling ring. The Duke was responsible for me ending up on the floor of that bus station. He'd destroyed my life after I refused to throw a fight. After I dug myself back up out of that hole, I devoted everything to bringing The Duke's family down by any means necessary. Henry Nutter was the first big victory of my war, and one that would surely not go without reprisal.

After that fight in the club, I couldn't let George go to the Washington women's penitentiary. A pretty girl like her wouldn't have lasted a day in there, especially being one of Nutter's old flames. The Duke's enemies tended to disappear in there, and the cops didn't ask too many questions about another crazy woman getting shivved.

Expecting and hoping that my appointment would be a distraught housewife with a cheating husband and a burning desire to get back at him, I had risen halfway to my feet to greet the imaginary woman when two men pushed past George and burst into the room. Two plainclothes gumshoes with their coat collars pulled up high against the miserable February cold outside.

"Augustus Saint." It wasn't a question. I didn't recognize the squared-jawed lead dick, but he seemed to know me. My reputation tended to precede me. The handsome detective whipped off his gloves and tossed them onto my desk like he owned the place. The two clowns were tracking mud behind them like careless children.

I called to George: "Hey baby, can you get in here and mop up the floor?"

"Screw you," she replied in a charming sing-song voice.

The dick was pissed. "Excuse me? Are you listening to me? And why are you muttering to yourself? You are Augustus Saint, right?"

"I might be. Depends on who's asking."

"Detective Shackleton, Mount Vernon P.D. This is my partner Detective Ely."

"Damn. I was hoping you were asking for a broad."

"Yeah, you really like the ladies, don't you Saint? I bet that gets you into all kinds of trouble."

I remembered the dame who got me drunk and tied me naked to a lamp post in downtown San Francisco with peanut butter smeared all over my junk. I was there for two days before anyone bothered to help me—besides stray dogs, that is—they all assumed I was some kind of avant-garde art installation. I nodded in agreement. "You have no idea."

"Why did you mumble to yourself like that before answering the question?" asked Ely. I recognized Ely by the enormous mole on his chin that looked like a small rodent trying to swallow his face. I often saw him at the coffee shop outside the police department down on Continental, frightening young children who thought a spider had laid eggs in his neck.

Shackleton looked me up and down slowly with his smoldering eyes and grunted. "Did you say something about spiders? Whatever. What do you know about a girl named Jillian Williams?"

I answered honestly. "I have no idea who you're talking about."

Shackleton pulled a damp manila envelope out from his overcoat and tossed a couple of pictures onto my desk. One showed a cute brunette with a short, almost boyish haircut. The other showed that same girl, standing right next to me in the front row at the boxing match last week, my arm around her waist.

"You want to reconsider your answer?" Shackleton asked. "Without the commentary under your breath?"

I wante— *Ahem* "Yeah, I know her. Didn't know her name though. I hooked up with her after the show. What's the big deal?"

"Miss Williams is enrolled at the Hospitality and

Tourism program at Skagit Valley College. She's also a fine amateur boxer, according to the boys on the circuit. But she hasn't been to any of her classes or to the gym in a week and no one's heard anything from her. Her friends got worried, so someone convinced her landlord to let them into her apartment. Know what they found?"

I didn't like where this was going. "Jillian?"

"Nope. But they found blood. A lot of it. And since you were the last person to see her, we've got a few questions for you."

"Am I under arrest?"

"Not yet. But we'd like you to come downtown for some questioning. You are, as they say, a very interesting person to this case."

This was bad. Very bad. The girl could be fine; maybe she just had a *really* bad visit from Aunt Flo and was so embarrassed she skipped town rather than tell her landlord about the mess. Though I had seen that very occurrence at least twice before, I doubted that was the case here. I remembered the girl—barely, I'm usually pretty drunk at the matches to dull the effect of the unpleasant violence unfolding between the ropes on my delicate stomach—but I certainly didn't have anything to do with her disappearance. Sure, maybe I got a bit excited when my bet on the preliminary bout paid off in spades and I showered her with drinks and bodily fluids, but that was it. We might have done some stuff that was illegal in a few states, but she was breathing when I snuck out the next morning.

Problem was, I *had* been in her apartment. They would find proof of that. And I couldn't account for my whereabouts for at least 24 hours after the show. With all the excitement and the extra cash from the bookie in my pocket, I may have fallen off the wagon a little bit. Okay, maybe a lot. They say the road to recovery is a lifelong journey, and I've got a terrible sense of direction.

When I left Jillian's place I seem to recall going to Burger King or maybe Papa John's, but when I woke up at midnight a day later I was lying on a bench at the bus station with no shoes and no wallet. George was pissed when I had to call her to come get me. If they put the girl's disappearance—or worse, death— at some time during my blackout I was up the river without a...you know, a rowing stick.

"You done yet?" Shackleton asked.

"Almost."

But what happened to the girl? I was *almost* positive that I didn't have anything to do with it, but it was awfully convenient that the girl I hooked up with disappears a few hours later with all fingers pointing at me. Especially when I'm still in the middle of sniffing out a major crime ring. It was a long shot to say this was all somehow connected to the Duke, but something was fishier than a cheap dock prostitute with a yeast infection.

"To hell with this," Ely grumbled. "He can talk to himself in the car."

They led me out of the office and I went along willingly, too lost in my thoughts to protest. Was this whole scheme about me, or had I just stumbled onto something much bigger? Was someone trying to get me out of the picture?

George looked at me with concern on her gorgeous mug as they brought me past her desk. I wondered if she was worried about me, or the fact that she would never get what she really wanted and secretly craved—that unspoken lust that simmered between us but we knew we could never act upon because we were both professionals—

"I heard that!" she screamed at me as they led me out the door and down the hall.

* * *

In case you were wondering, the fist was still coming at my face. It had traveled about—oh, three or four inches during the time it took me to revisit that scene in the Mount Vernon Police Station. I can think really fast when I'm in fighting mode. Almost as fast as back when I was snorting PCP like it was going out of style. Which, to be fair, it was. Does anyone do angel dust anymore? I'm afraid to ask, because my second question will inevitably be "Can you get me some?"

The second hand hadn't moved, though. I was still waiting for the "tock."

* * *

"What happened to the girl?" Shackleton said for what seemed like the twentieth time in the last ten minutes. I assumed they were playing "good cop, bad cop," and that Shackleton was the "good cop."

"I told you, I don't know," I said, for what seemed like the eighteenth time. The first two times I had just told them to screw off, which as you can imagine hadn't gone over well. "I went home with her, we fooled around, and at some point in the night I snuck out. I was drunk, I don't remember what time it was, but she was alive when I left and all her blood was still inside her body."

"You sure about that?" Shackleton said. "Would you swear that in court?"

I shrugged. Was that a trick question? I assumed swearing in court was frowned upon...

"What exactly did you do to her, Saint?" said Shackleton's partner, Ely. He would be the "bad cop" in this scene, though I had trouble taking him seriously because that mole on his chin was the size of small European country. Latvia, maybe? The first couple times I had seen him I assumed he had somehow wiped feces on his face, but from close up I could see the ugly hairs on it.

38

"Exactly? I didn't take you for the kind that got off on kinky stories, Ely." I shrugged. "I'll tell you if you want, but I'm really going to have trouble making it sexy while I'm staring at that disgusting thing growing on your chin."

"Shut up, Saint." He made a move as if he were going to punch me. I didn't flinch. I was used to getting pummeled in the face by guys twice Ely's size.

"You're getting better." Shackleton took a drag on his cigarette. "I can barely see your lips moving now while you're narrating."

"Thanks, I was practicing in the car. So am I under arrest or what? I've got a business to run, you know, clients to see, cheating husbands to spy on..."

"Oh, you talking about this?" Ely slapped a sheet of paper on the table in front of me.

"Is that my private investigator's license?"

"This is not an investigator's license. This is a dog license, and everywhere it says 'canine' you whited it out and wrote 'Private Dick.'"

"Damn. I'm going to have to have a long talk with my secretary."

There was a knock at the door. Shackleton went over and spoke briefly with someone I couldn't see. Ely sat on the edge of the table and made mean faces at me. Or maybe he was flirting, I'm not certain. The stupid mole was distracting.

"Well, we've been told we can't hold you any longer without pressing charges," Shackleton said as he returned, flipping through a file folder.

"So, you're charging me with...?"

"I should charge you with operating without a private investigator's license, but your tip brought down Nutter so I'll let it slide. Besides that..." His voice trailed off. "We've got nothing. The CSI nerds came back and said the blood stains in Jillian Williams' room weren't hers and were splattered there several hours after you claim you left. And we have witnesses that vouch for your whereabouts during that time."

"You do?"

Shackleton grunted and tossed the file on the table. "Get the hell out of here. You're off the hook for now, but if I get even a whiff of you running your little scam business or if Jillian turns up dead, I'll come down on your ass so hard it'll make your head spin."

I stood up and grabbed my coat from the back of the chair. "In my experience, my ass is pretty resilient."

"Yeah, well we'll find out exactly how resilient if you keep messing with The Duke. Watch out for yourself, Saint."

* * *

The fist collided with my jaw. I registered the impact critically, like a craftsman admiring a fine piece of furniture. It was well-thrown, with a good shoulder behind it and a little bit of hip and torso twist for that extra oomph. It landed perfectly, the first two knuckles of the hand focusing the energy exquisitely into my first and second bicuspids. I felt one of the premolars crack at the root and knew that I would be spitting it out in a few moments.

A damn fine punch, all in all. I had been hit harder, but not much. That was at least a nine-out-of-ten.

I had trouble getting my bearings. My senses misfired for a moment, like the punch had knocked something loose in my brain. I knew someone was yelling at me but all I could hear was the "tick-tock-tick-tock" of the clock on the wall behind my attacker's head. Four whole seconds passed before the bastard took another swing.

I will spare you the explicit details of the next blow, but let me say it was just as expertly-landed as the first. This one struck a little higher on my cheek and probably cracked my zygomatic bone.

40

* * *

I left the station to find a familiar face waiting for me in Washington's cold February rain. Axl Rose take note: February rain is way worse than anything they have in November. It was already dark, and George was standing in the light of a street lamp under a big, black umbrella. She shivered in the cold, with just a hint of blond hair peeking out from under a knit cap and a fetching length of leg below a deep green pea coat.

She threw her arms around me without thinking, hugging my neck tighter than some back alley thugs who've tried to choke me out. George realized what she was doing and disentangled herself, though her scent lingered like a welcome ghost on my coat for hours afterward.

She punched me in the arm. "What the hell is wrong with you? What did you do to that girl?"

"Nothing!"

She cocked her head and glared at me.

"Okay, well lots, technically. But I had nothing to do with her disappearance."

She pouted and glared for another moment before stepping close to me again, sharing the coverage of the umbrella. We started to walk away down the slick, dark street. We had no particular destination in mind.

"You're lucky I believe you. Otherwise I wouldn't have told them you were with me that day."

"So, it was you." I had suspected it was, but it wasn't true of course. I hadn't seen George that entire day until she picked me up at the bus station across town, but her lie had saved my neck. "Why did you do it?"

She took my arm as we walked. It was strange— she wasn't usually so touchy-feely. "You gave me a job when Henry kicked me out. Might have kept me

41

from getting deported."

"It wasn't a favour. I needed a secretary. And I pay you for your work."

"You do—a hell of a lot, actually. Do you know what a secretary is supposed to make?"

"Not a clue."

"Never mind. My salary is right in the middle of the range."

She laughed. It was a beautiful sound, and one I had never remembered hearing before. Usually she was so distant, so cool. I'm not sure if she was like that before Nutter, or if whatever happened between them had hardened her. I liked it, but it was unsettling. Something had changed. Which made me lying to her feel ever worse.

"Look, doll, I mean George, I have to tell you something. I was the one who turned in Henry Nutter. It's my fault he went down."

George didn't bat a single one of her long black eyelashes. "I know. I was the one who slipped that envelope full of evidence under your door."

I stopped dead in my tracks. "That was you?"

"Who the hell did you think it was? The evidence fairy?"

Honestly, I had no idea. I have so many blackouts from various concussions and benders that I usually don't question when unexplained persons or objects show up in my office. "But...wasn't he good to you? I mean, you could have gotten locked up yourself or sent away."

She looked down, unable to meet my gaze. "He was good enough, for a while. But he was bad sometimes. And he was very bad to other people. I couldn't let it go on any longer. I couldn't live with myself."

She looked up and smiled. I felt a weird feeling in my chest, similar to that time I got shot point-blank by a .22. "You're a good guy, Saint. Under all the bluster and the booze and the womanizing, there's a good guy trying to get out." She put her hand on my chest to punctuate her words and I nearly fell over. "There are a lot of bad people in this world. Someone needs to stand up to them."

"I'm not a hero..."

"Not yet. I've watched you these last few weeks. You are without a doubt the worst detective in the world. Actually, I don't think you're even really a detective. But you're not doing this for money or for some weird creepy reasons I wouldn't put past you. You're looking to do the right thing. You have a good heart. Don't let the bad guys of the world break you down."

"They broke me a long time ago, doll."

For the first time, she didn't correct me when I called her that. Instead she just smiled and kissed me on the cheek.

"See you around, Gussy." She started to walk away, leaving me holding the umbrella.

"Where are you going?" I called after her. She just smiled, turned around and kept walking. I was too dumbfounded to follow her. I watched her walk through the rain half a block down the street before disappearing around a corner.

* * *

I was still daydreaming about George and her magical legs when I walked into my apartment a half hour later, looking for a shower and the half-bottle of rum under the kitchen sink. A hit of meth would have been better; it was times like this I was extra bummed that I'd given up hard drugs. Something about talking to cops always got me jonsin' for god's beautiful rock.

What I was not looking for was Jillian Williams, who I found sitting on a dining room chair in my living room with a handgun pointed at my chest.

43

I took off my jacket and coat as cool as I could, hoping she couldn't tell that I had wet myself a little bit. "Why didn't you just sit in the easy chair, sweetheart?"

"Because it smells like someone died on it."

I nodded. "Yeah, I found it in the alley, so that's entirely possible."

She stood up and walked toward me, the gun never wavering. She was dressed in black stretch pants and a plain grey sweater. Normally I would have taken a moment to admire a woman's gait in tight pants, but something about the piece in her hand threw off my usual routine. I did note that she didn't have that hypnotic sway that George employed; she walked with conviction and purpose. Her steps were decisive and surprisingly nimble. She walked like a fighter.

"The cops are looking for you."

That's when she punched me, sending my world spiraling into a series of flashbacks as to how the hell I got here. Christ, that woman hit like a freight train. What did she need a gun for?

The first punch got me so hard that I left myself completely open for the second and soon found myself on the floor.

"What the hell was that?" she demanded, standing over me like a conquering warrior.

"My tooth hitting the laminate flooring." I spat blood on her black, steel-toed boots.

"No, after I hit you the first time you started blabbering like a nut job. I thought you used to be a fighter. I couldn't have scrambled your brain that bad with one punch."

"Just caught me off guard. Forgot myself for a minute. I'll try to keep the narration internal from now on."

She shook her head, thin lips pursed above her strong jaw. "I thought you were acting so weird that

44

night we hooked up because you were drunk. But it looks like you're always crazy."

"That's what my therapist says."

She laughed. It wasn't a pleasant sound. "You don't seem the type to go in for a shrink."

"Oh, don't worry, it was court-ordered."

She put the gun against my head. It wasn't the first time I'd felt the cool metal of a barrel against my skull, and I kinda hoped it wouldn't be my last. "You don't remember me, do you?"

"Of course I do. I might have been drunk, but trust me, it was a memorable night even if the details are fuzzy."

She cracked me in the head with the butt of the handgun and I nearly blacked out. I really needed to stop leaving myself open. "That wasn't the first time we met, you moron. Don't you remember another club, a couple of months ago?"

"Sister, if I step into a club I don't usually leave it until I'm unconscious..."

And then it hit me. Well, yes, she hit me again, too, but more importantly the memory of where I had seen her before slammed into me nearly as hard as her fist. As I lay on the floor, watching the seconds tick away on that big clock behind her head, I flashed back to watching two girls rolling around on a dance floor, clawing and kicking at each other.

"You were the girl that George beat up," I managed through bloody teeth. "But...you fight like a beast. You should have killed her."

"I let her beat me up. I wanted her to go to jail. And I don't want your narration about it!"

"Okay, just give me a second to clear my head. It's hard to keep it internal when you keep punching like that."

I shook my head a few times to clear out the cobwebs. Did she hear me? She was staring at me like I was a dog that had whizzed on her leg, but she wasn't registering or reacting to my words. That was good. "Better?" I asked.

"Yeah. Can I kill you now?"

"Just a second."

Why did she want George to go to jail? Was she hoping she would turn into a lesbian like some sort of *Orange is the New Black* scenario? No wait, that was my fantasy. What could a random woman in a bar gain by sending George to Washington Women's Pen?

Unless it wasn't random.

Because she knew that if George ended up in the slammer, she could be quietly offed, and no one would ask too many questions. The same way they could make me disappear if I was arrested for Jillian's murder. Washington State Penitentiaries were basically The Duke's garbage disposal for his enemies.

"You were the bit on the side." I slowly rose to my feet, staggering just slightly more than I needed to, hanging harder on my ugly shag curtains than strictly necessary. "The one that Nutter left George for."

She rolled her eyes. "You dumbass. I'm his sister."

I nearly choked. "Really? I thought he was a Brit, not a hillbilly."

"I'm not...why are you so frustrating?"

"Most people call it charming. If you're his sister, why don't you talk all funny like he and George does?" I kept swaying, praying to god that she thought I was still woozy. And couldn't hear me talking to myself.

"Half-sister, technically. Mom moved to the States with me when I was a baby. But when I grew up I kept in touch with Henry. He was the only one in my family who didn't treat me like some kind of embarrassment. I loved him. And your bitch girlfriend put him in jail."

"Two things: One, George is my secretary, not my

girlfriend. Yet."

She smiled. "What's number two?"

"Two is you should have killed me a minute ago."

I made my move and stepped outside her gun hand faster than she was expecting, though unfortunately a fraction of a second slower than I had hoped. The gun went off and I felt a shot of fire across my arm. Screaming, I grabbed her right arm, probably breaking it in the process, and slammed her face-first into that big ugly clock on the wall behind her. The glass shattered and she went limp, sliding down to the floor and leaving very horror-movie-esque streaks of blood across the clock face.

I hate hitting women. I also hated how we were perpetuating the misogynistic stereotype in every Mickey Spillane novel of the bad guy being a woman.

But there it was, the mystery of Jillian Williams solved with miss Williams lying in a pool of blood on my apartment floor instead of her own. I'm not sure if that was much better. My own blood was running down my arm and mixing with hers, intermingling one final set of bodily fluids I don't think we crossed that fateful night a week ago. At least I was alive, and Williams had admitted she was crazier than a cat tossed off a bridge in a pillowcase. Now it was just a matter of making it stick in court.

I was bringing down The Duke, one lowlife at a time. Every piece of his empire that I broke was revenge for a piece of my life he had taken away. I might not be a real private dick yet—the certification from Skagit Valley College was in the mail, I swear—but I wasn't going to let that stop me.

I lit a cigarette as I watched the seconds tick by on the shattered clock. The Duke's time was running out. I smiled and brought the smoke to my lips, then yelped and dropped it when Jillian stirred. I kicked her in the head and went to look for my phone.

I decided I should probably call the cops to come clean this up.

The End

C.D. wrote his first story when he was five years old, and he made his baby-sitter look up how to spell "extra-terrestrial" in the dictionary. He now writes stories about un-heroic people doing generally hilarious things in horrifying worlds. A loving husband and proud father of two wonderful little kids, C.D. was born and raised in Newfoundland and currently resides in Ottawa, Ontario. There was also a ten-year period in between where he tried to make a go of a career in theatre in Toronto, but we don't talk about that.
www.cdgallantking.ca
www.twitter.com/cdgallantking
www.facebook.com/cdgallantking

The Tide Waits
By Rebecca M. Douglass

"**S**hut it, you sotted fool!"

"It's th' lord's truth."

The thump of a blow cut off the too-loud declaration, and Lira looked up from the glass she had just filled. In the back corner of the bar, two shepherds lambasted one another drunkenly. Sighing, she handed the glass across to the blacksmith, and picked up the stout club she kept to maintain the peace. Crossing the room in three strides, Lira grabbed the loudmouth by the collar, and barred the second man from further attack with her weapon.

Lira dragged the dazed shepherd to the door, pushed him out into the night, and turned to confront his drinking buddy and sparring partner. "You, too. Out."

The second shepherd cast a forlorn look at the table where half a glass of ale still stood. "Aw, I was just—" He took another look at the bartender's face, shut up, and went out into the night.

Arthur and Owain were old friends; Lira knew it was safe to throw them out together. They might finish their fight but they'd do no lasting harm, and out there they wouldn't break up her furniture.

Lira glanced around before closing the door. Just about full dark. This time of year, that meant it was going on for eleven. Pretty soon, she could chase out the last of the drinkers and shut down for the night. Turing back to the lantern-lit room, Lira gave the blacksmith a look that moved him to gulp half his remaining ale. Two or three other men did likewise, whether from fear of Lira or of the wives who would scold them for staying abroad late, she didn't know and didn't care.

Not waiting for the bartender's call of "drink up and get out!" the quiet man at the table in the far corner rose and headed for the door. Lira took a hard look at him as he brushed past her without a nod. He had been drinking stronger drink than the locals but appeared steady enough. Lira didn't like strangers in her bar, and she didn't trust men who wanted "something better" than what everyone else was drinking.

* * *

The village at the back of the narrow cove wouldn't see the sun for an hour or two, shaded as it was by the bulk of land to the east. But there was light enough for the fishermen who loaded their nets and pushed the small fleet out through the gentle surf that washed the beach. They turned their bows to the sea, most hoisting sails.

Huw fished alone, and his small skiff ran best on oars. He rowed steadily out of the harbor and turned away from the others. By all the signs learned in decades of fishing this coast, he thought they'd be biting best in the lee of Goblin's Head.

That lone rock island stood a hundred feet offshore. The stone arch that had once bridged it to the mainland was now a rocky anchor chain washed by the high tides. It had fallen when Huw's grandfather was a boy, and the fish liked the pockets of calm it created. Huw rowed toward the jutting head for a few minutes, until the shrieking of gulls made him stop rowing and turn for a better look. The birds were attacking something on the largest rock at the base of Goblin's Head.

Probably a dead seal or some such. Huw steered his boat closer. At low tide, man or beast could cross dry-shod to the island, and the base of the massive

50

sea-stack was surrounded by rocks shed from its sides and exposed by the retreat of the water. Curiosity drew him nearer, along with the idea that a fresh seal might be skinned and the fur sold. He would have to hurry, though, if he wanted to collect the carcass. The tide was rising fast, and the rock would soon be under water.

Huw couldn't land next to the carcass. The waves surged unpredictably and too many rocks waited to rip the bottom of a careless man's boat. Huw pulled for the land side of the Head instead, where the stones of the long-collapsed land bridge still stood above the waves. There he managed to scramble ashore, holding the boat by the painter. He found a weathered tree growing above the splash line and tied off his skiff. Then Huw studied the distance between himself and what he no longer thought was a seal.

The incoming tide made it a tricky scramble around the base of Goblin's Head, but not impossible. He moved from rock to rock with deliberate speed, not haste; to injure himself here would mean death as the incoming tide swept over the rocks. On this morning, he was safe until about a half hour after the sun rose—and that sun now lit the top of the Head.

Like most of the villagers, Huw had been atop the sea stack many times. But this time he didn't mount the steep, half-scrambling route up the rock. He had climbed it enough times in his youth, like all the others who had helped to carve the path, whistling at the danger to prove their manhood. More than one had died for that proof. Climbing around the base on the rocks the Goblin had shed wasn't a whole lot safer.

Death had visited Goblin's Head once again. Huw reached the body that sprawled on the rock, and took in the rough homespun pants and coat before lifting the man's shoulder to look at the face. He knew the man.

Decades of gutting fish and mourning those lost at sea had hardened the old fisherman. What he saw made him regret his breakfast, but experience won and the meal stayed put. Huw let the body drop back, hiding the hideous slash across Arthur's throat and the face crushed by a fall. He looked around, realizing that that there was no one to help. The other boats stood well out to sea now, lines and nets in the water. Even if someone saw him, they would not leave their fishing, and none could arrive in time to help if they did.

The poor man couldn't be left for the gulls to pick at until he washed out to sea. Already the waves were getting closer. Huw bent, and with the strength built from decades of pulling fish, lifted the lifeless man and laid him across his shoulders. He staggered and skidded as he carried the corpse back over the jumble of rocks. Losing his footing on a sea-slickened boulder, Huw nearly dropped his burden. If it hadn't been a calm day, the passage would have been impossible. As it was, it taxed his strength, and Huw reached his skiff with a sigh of relief.

Then came the challenge of getting the body into the boat, and he struggled for some minutes before Arthur lay in the bottom of the skiff. Huw pushed off from the rocks and scrambled to his place at the oars, pulling away from the dangerous shore before taking a moment to cover the dead man's ruined face with his kerchief. Trying not to think about a lost morning's fishing, he began the long pull back to the village.

* * *

Lira stirred in her sleep. The noises in her dream gradually merged with the waking sounds, until she realized that someone was pounding on her door—not the front of the tavern, but the back door that led to the private room where she slept. Or didn't sleep, as was now the case.

Sitting up, Lira swung her legs out of bed, shoved her feet into the boots that stood ready, and crossed to the door, indifferent to the indecency of appearing in her nightshirt. Someone needed putting in his place. It was barely dawn, by all the gods, and she'd gone to bed too few hours since. She ignored the streaks of sunlight across her floor; even an hour or two past sunup was the crack of dawn to a bartender. She yanked open the door.

"What the devil do you want with me?" The words were out before her mind sorted out the face of the old fisherman. Huw. He should have been out with the fish, not here disturbing her sleep.

"There's been murder done."

There weren't many things Huw could have said that would have stopped Lira's wrath at having her sleep disturbed. Those words did it, and her mind shifted gears at once.

"Who, when, where?" She didn't ask what he wanted with her. Everyone came to Lira when trouble hit the village. Though there was a squire in the big house once more, he was an outsider.

"The sheepman Arthur, at Goblin's Head, sometime between midnight and sunup. Body's in my skiff." Huw jerked his chin toward the beach.

Lira nodded. She understood the time frame he'd laid out. She'd been up the Head a time or two herself and knew it could only be reached when the tide was at least halfway out.

"I'll come," she said as she closed the door and went to dress. She pulled on breeches and shirt. This was no time for skirts, not for examining dead bodies and scrambling over the rocks for clues.

The old fisherman still stood patiently outside her door when she opened it a few minutes later. As soon as she appeared, he started down to the beach, where a length of canvas covered a small boat pulled well above the high tide line.

When she folded back the canvas, Lira recognized the body even without seeing the face. She'd gripped that collar only a few hours earlier, to propel the wearer thereof out the door of her bar.

"Yes, that's Arthur," she said as she reached to uncover the dead man's face. "I suppose he and Owain continued their fight and things went too far." She drew in a sharp breath at the sight of the damaged head and scowled at the great slash across the throat.

"I don't reckon this was a fight between friends." Huw summed up both their thoughts.

"Tell me again where you found him."

"On the rocks at the base of Goblin's Head. The gulls drew me."

"His clothes are dry." That was true, except where they had gotten wet in Huw's efforts to salvage the body or from the water in the bottom of the skiff.

"He didn't drown," Huw interpreted. "He fell."

Lira glanced toward Goblin's Head and nodded. "From the Head. But by the looks of this, he was dead enough before he fell—or was thrown."

"Aye. And the body meant to be washed out to sea and maybe never found, but the killer didn't know the tides."

"I think," Lira said, "that we will have to notify the new squire. This man was alive enough when I threw him out of the bar last night." She winced at her own choice of words.

Huw echoed Lira's wince. "If I go for Squire, it'll cost me my day's catch," he grumbled. He caught Lira's eye and muttered "I know. 'Twas I who found him. I'm going."

* * *

At the big house, it took Huw far too long to get a

response. Didn't these people know that the day was half over by sunrise, let alone by this hour? Already the day was growing warm. How could they still be sleeping? Huw hammered on the door again, until at last someone opened it to stare down at him from the top step.

"What do you want?" The supercilious question annoyed the fisherman.

"There's been murder done," Huw grunted. "I plucked the corpse from the shore this morning. Squire'll need to see to things."

The footman or whatever he was seemed taken aback. "My lord is abed. He was abroad late, returning from a visit to another of his manors. Surely you don't expect him to rise at the crack of dawn to see to," he sniffed in distaste, "the results of peasant brawls, and him at Willowby until the small hours."

"When murder's been done, it's Squire's job to see things set right." Not that Huw had much hope of it in this case. A bunch of foolish outsiders, come from who knew where and with no love for either the village or the sea. He'd tell his story as he must, but for justice, he had more faith in Lira.

* * *

The sun was halfway to noon, and the tide ebbing, before Squire Randolfus finally rode into the yard of the Golden Jug, his man at his side. Lira and Huw had carried the body of Arthur into the woodshed and sent a pair of boys to find Owain.

Randolfus dismounted, his face reflecting not pity for the dead man but irritation at this intrusion into his day. A small crowd of villagers had left their work to discuss the murder, but they fell silent when the squire arrived.

"I have returned but a few hours since from my manor at Willowby. I fail to see why I should be roused from my sleep to resolve a case of a drunken brawl with a bad end," he said, his long nose pinched either with with distaste at the whole affair or at the smells that had begun to rise in the woodshed as the day warmed.

"It's your responsibility," Lira said. Her patience, already worn thin by lack of sleep and long waiting, cracked at this callous indifference to the loss of a life.

"Very well." The squire brushed a bit of dust from his sleeve, glanced at the dead man, and returned to the fresher air outside before asking, "Who was he?"

"The shepherd Arthur," Lira answered, and several villagers nodded confirmation. The squire's attendant tried to disperse the watchers, but they weren't going.

"When was he last seen alive?" Randolfus asked the question of anyone who would answer.

People looked from one to another and shrugged. Then they parted to make way for Owain, accompanied by the carter Dai. The shepherd's face looked drained of blood, at the shock of the news or from some other fear, or maybe the effects of too much ale the night before.

"I left him," he faltered. "After Lira tossed us out he wouldn't come to his bed. I thought he would sleep it off in some barn or haystack. He was too drunk and we both too weary for more fighting. I left him," he repeated, "and went to my own bed."

"To your bed? And did you stay there?" Randolfus demanded.

"No." A murmur ran through the crowd at this confession. Owain added, "I was called back out before I had more than just gone to bed, to see to Dai's horse. She was bad with the colic."

"Aye," confirmed Dai, a stolid villager of middle age. "He's been with me and my Nellie all night, since sometime around the midnight hour."

Lira hoped they'd saved the horse. Dai needed the

animal, and Lira needed the goods they delivered.

The squire ignored Owain and Dai to demand of the crowd, "Did anyone else see the dead man last night?"

Of course someone did, Lira thought. But that person wouldn't be likely to say so.

One of Randolfus's attendants stepped forward to look at the corpse. Lira recognized the drinker who had demanded "something better" the night before. So that was who the stranger was. As the squire's right-hand man he thought he was above drinking the ale the villagers enjoyed. He studied the dead face, apparently unmoved by the bloody void beneath the chin.

"Have you seen him, Alain?" Randolfus asked with more patience than he'd shown so far.

"Yes," Alain said, with the hesitation of one who does not yet know the locals well. He turned on Lira. "You threw him out of the bar last night, along with his friend here."

"I did," she confirmed. That was no news to any villager.

"Though," the man turned narrowed eyes on Owain, "you looked scarcely friendly last night."

Owain shrugged. "He says foolish things when he's drunk. He angered me."

Lira narrowed her own eyes. She knew Owain well enough to know he wasn't telling the whole truth. Never mind. She'd have it out of him when she got him alone.

Alain went on. "I saw them as I left here last night. I heard two men fighting on yon path." He pointed to the track leading to the open fields. "When I drew near, I could see enough to know it for these shepherds, continuing their argument."

Randolfus turned on Owain, who stared back in fright and confusion. Lira kept her gaze on Alain, suspicious of a story that so neatly trapped the nearest suspect.

"They must have fought more bitterly than I knew, and this one threw his mate into the sea in hopes of not being discovered," Alain concluded.

Huw opened his mouth, but at a look from Lira, closed it again.

Alain added, "I am sorry I didn't interfere, but how was I to know? The poor man must have been slain after I rode on." He didn't sound very concerned.

Randolfus pointed at Owain. "There is your killer, then. He slew his mate in a drunken rage, and threw him from the cliffs. Take him," he ordered.

Before Alain could move, Lira and Huw took Owain by the arms. "We will hold him, Squire Randolfus," Lira said. "We would not have your household put out of countenance for a mere shepherd." The squire didn't appear to hear the sarcasm in her words, but the villagers did, and murmured approval.

"He should be locked up in the manor," Randolfus began, but as the villagers closed ranks around their own, he quieted. He appeared satisfied with seeing the man locked in a room in the back of the Golden Jug. He tested the door to be certain before he and his men mounted and left, with the order that Owain was to be left strictly alone.

* * *

Lira watched Randolfus and his men until they were well down the road out of the village, before turning to Huw. "Well, there rides a liar," she said.

Huw nodded. "That Alain lied about the time Arthur died, Lira, and it was a lie only a stranger could tell."

She nodded. "When did the tide turn last night?"

The old fisherman considered. "The low was about three hours past midnight. I had to row against the coming tide this morning, and it was nearly over the

58

rocks before I got yon shepherd into my boat."

Lira considered that. "It must have been near eleven when I kicked those boys out of the tavern."

Neither of them commented further. The tide would have rendered Goblin's Head inaccessible for an hour or more after the shepherds' precipitate departure from the tavern. If it was Alain who had killed Arthur up there, he must have known that. But they hadn't said Arthur had fallen from the rocks, only that he'd been plucked from the shore. Goblin's Head and the importance of the tide was their secret—theirs, and the killer's.

Owain was in Dai's stable with the unhappy Nellie well before midnight. Arthur might have been dead before Dai came looking for help with his horse, but the corpse could not have been thrown from Goblin's Head until midnight or even closer to one in the morning. And Lira had little faith that he had been killed elsewhere and carried to the Head to be thrown into the sea, though she would have to visit the Head to be sure he had died there.

Huw scratched his head. "There's another odd thing," he said. "When I went to the manor just now, the fellow who opened the door told me that his lord had returned late from visiting another manor."

"Yes, that's what Randolfus said as well."

"His chief man, this Alain, is always with him when he rides out, but last night he was in your tavern drinking."

"And in no hurry to leave until I showed those two the door," Lira mused. "Then he ups and shoves his way out. But to spend the evening drinking is not like a man whose master has demanded he ride with him, and still less like one who should have been with him at a distant manor."

"Someone in that lot is lying," Huw said.

"So they all are," said a voice at Lira's shoulder,

an old woman whose name escaped her.

"What do you know, Grandmother?" Lira asked.

"I work at the manor, there," the woman said. "In the kitchen. And the lord was there, sitting before his fire, when I left at sunset. But I tell you, his boots were wet this morning." She spoke low, so the onlookers could not hear what she said, but Lira heard, and understood.

The old woman disappeared into the crowd, in a hurry to put herself out of sight after her testimony.

"So Randolfus was not at some distant manor," Lira mused, "But he went out late and returned with wet boots." By the time she finished considering this, Huw had gone. He had fish to catch.

Still thinking, Lira went into her tavern, to the storeroom where they had locked up Owain. She opened the door and looked him over. "I think," she said, "you had best tell me what you and Arthur fought over."

The shepherd gulped, swallowed, and made up his mind.

"He was talkin' loose, Lira."

"About what?" She tried to be patient.

"About the squire," Owain whispered, so low she had to lean in close enough to be assaulted by his vile breath. "I just wanted him to shut up before he got into trouble."

"So you weren't really fighting?"

"No! He was my friend! I hit him because it was the only way I could quiet him. He wouldn't stop talking about what he'd heard, and anyone might have been listening and carried word." Owain's voice dropped away to nothing, as he realized that someone must have done just that.

Lira kept her own voice low. "And what had he heard?"

Owain squirmed, avoided her gaze, and tried

to back away, but there was nowhere to go. Finally he leaned in, put his lips practically in her ear, and breathed, "He heard that Squire is in league with the pirates. That he buys and sells for them."

Lira rocked back on her heels, head reeling. No wonder Owain was afraid. And, she thought, her mind moving fast, no wonder Squire Randolfus had ordered no one should speak to him. Owain would have to be silenced, and quickly.

Randolfus needed Arthur dead, but who had done the murder? Not Owain. Alain was her best suspect, or the lord himself. If Alain had heard what Arthur announced so carelessly over his ale, he could have taken care of the matter himself, or gone to tell his lord. If Alain had returned to the manor when he left the Golden Jug, Randolfus could have hunted for Arthur, slain him, and disposed of the body. She had no idea why Arthur had gone up Goblin's Head, though.

"He might have gone up there to watch," Owain said when she asked the question aloud.

"What do you mean?"

"He said he was going to prove the story, so maybe he went up the Head to watch for the pirates. It would be a good place," the shepherd acknowledged. "You can see most of the coast from up there, and once the tide's in, no one can sneak up on you."

"No. But the tide was out," Lira said.

Owain scratched his head. "Maybe he saw something and went to investigate?"

Alain could have watched to see where Arthur went, then fetched the squire. Or they might have lured him out to the Head, where they could do their deed in private.

She would have to climb the Head and search for evidence, however unlikely she was to find any. Lira opened the door and glanced into her kitchen.

Getting on for noon by the light. The path up Goblin's Head would be passable soon, if it weren't already. She needed to visit Arthur's hut, too.

Alain and Randolfus would be back in force to take Owain. He had heard Arthur's accusations, and they would want him silenced. No wonder they had pinned the crime on him, and no wonder they wanted him at the manor house. They needed a quick execution with no chance to talk, and they wouldn't wait long. In a detached way, she considered that she and Huw would be next on their list.

The church. It was the one place that could offer a safe sanctuary, she hoped. Pirates weren't overly pious, but Randolfus was trying to appear something else. He might be slow to violate sanctuary, slow enough to allow her to present proof. Then the villagers could serve up their own justice.

Lira opened the front door of the tavern, threw a bucket of water on the straggly flowers that grew in the foreyard, and looked up the road and around the village. No one was about. She stepped back in, grabbed Owain by the arm, and pulled him at a run across the square and into the church. No hooves hammered after them on the road. She had no doubt that they had been seen by the villagers, but they would defend the sanctuary of the church over the will of the new squire.

To the bewildered priest she ordered, "Give him sanctuary!" before she turned back to the outdoors, pausing at the last moment to cross herself in the general direction of the altar. It never hurt to honor the gods, whatever life might have taught you about belief.

Hurrying along the path toward the Head, she thought she heard the sound of horses on the road. Randolfus was coming back for Owain. The locks on the tavern and the storeroom would slow him, maybe enough.

Arthur's hut could wait. If Owain was right, the shepherd had not gone there in any case. Instead, Lira skidded down the path to the beach by Goblin's Head. The way over the rocks was still washed by waves, but not so deeply that a knowing local couldn't make it, though it was taking a chance. She timed her crossing, stepping lightly from rock to rock, avoiding the holes, and scrambled onto the Head ahead of a breaking wave. She remembered the way up, and mounted quickly to the summit. From there, she saw the riders, one veering off to the tavern, and one coming straight on to Goblin's Head. He wasn't coming because of her; he couldn't have seen her from the road. He had left some sign he now knew he needed to erase, and she had to find it.

It was easy to see where Arthur died. A slit throat made for a lot of blood, and the grasses were trampled as well. Arthur had fought, though not for long.

Lira checked her pursuer again. He had left his horse and was now half running, half sliding down to the shore. She turned to her search, and found what she sought: a lantern, kicked and broken in the struggle. It didn't prove Randolfus' guilt, though it was of a quality no one in the village could afford. It did prove that someone had signaled from the Head, either to the pirates, or to lure Arthur to his death.

The squire proved his own guilt with his frantic haste to reach Goblin's head, where no one but Lira and Huw—and the killer—knew the murder had taken place.

He was splashing through the waves now, stumbling and sliding over rocks still washed by the retreating tide. Lira watched as he rushed toward her. He wore sword and knife at his belt, and she had no weapon, and no way off the Head except through him, or off the side to die in the sea. By now he had seen her and knew that she held the key to his guilt, not only about the murder but about his connection to the pirates.

He hadn't killed the shepherd fast enough to silence him. Lira knew, and Owain knew, and soon everyone in the village would know that the new "squire" dealt with pirates. He wasn't a man of the sea himself, though, or he would have known better than to challenge the tide. Lira watched, stone-faced, as the man's elegant riding boots slipped on a wet rock, and he fell heavily off the raised line of rubble. Before he could find his feet, a rogue wave broke over the causeway. When the water receded, there was no sign of the man, nor of his heavy jeweled sword belt and knife.

Lira sat down to wait for the tide to fall.

The End

Rebecca M. Douglass is a writer of children's fiction, cozy mysteries, and fantasy. When not writing, she likes to spend her time hiking, biking, and traveling with her husband. She works at the local library, where she hopes to learn the secrets of the Ninja Librarian.
www.ninjalibrarian.com
www.facebook.com/RebeccaDouglassNinjaLibrarian
www.twitter.com/Douglass_RM

The Little Girl in the Bayou
J. R. Ferguson

Mack Crawford walked into the Moss Bayou Police Department. The officer behind the desk glanced up but quickly returned his attention to the crossword puzzle on his desk.

"Excuse me, I'd like to talk with one of your detectives," Mack said.

The officer took a deep breath, then shook his head as if dealing with a complete idiot. "I decide who you talk to. What's your problem?"

Mack gritted his teeth. He knew better than to get on the bad side of small town law enforcement. He took a picture from his shirt pocket and held it up for the officer to see. Riddled with water spots and slightly faded from the sun, it clearly showed a young girl wrapped in fish net. Even though the child was fully dressed in shorts and a tee shirt, the picture portrayed a horrible, sinister image.

The officer swallowed hard. "What's your name, buddy, and where'd you get this?"

"Mack Crawford. Found it near the bayou over at City Park when I was putting a boat in the water."

"You need to see the Chief."

He motioned for Mack to follow him back to a corner office. "Chief. This guy's got a picture here he *says* he found in the bayou."

The police chief was a large, solid man with hair that resembled a Mohawk and came to a widow's peak on his forehead. He ran his tongue over his front teeth while he studied Mack from across his desk. "You from around here?"

"I work for ArkLaTex Construction. Been here

almost two years."

"Yeah, lots of you people around. Taking our jobs and taking our women."

Mack said nothing. He was used to the remark. He'd worked on a number of projects across the state of Louisiana and always heard the same thing. The chief glanced at the picture, frowned, then tossed it on his cluttered desk. "Looks bad. Say you found it floatin' in the bayou?"

"On the bank. Probably hadn't been there all that long. Thought you might check into it."

The chief nodded. "And how do you suggest I do that?"

The question took Mack by surprise. He didn't answer. Safe thing to do would be to wait for the chief to continue.

"Who knows how old it is. Looks like it's printed out on someone's home computer. Besides, could be anything. Kidnapping. Even a movie production." He shrugged. "Could be parents trying to bring in some extra cash. Times are hard."

He leaned back in his chair. His shirt was wrinkled, sweaty. It clung to his chest.

Mack stared. "I don't think it's that old. Are you saying you aren't going to check it out?"

The chief squirmed. "Sure, we'll check it out. Soon as we can." He inhaled, as if he had the weight of the world on his shoulders. "You probably know the Mayor is trying to do away with my department. Sheriff's office wants to take it over." He rubbed his hand across his face. "Feels like a swamp full of gators stalking me. Most of my boys are spending their time looking for other jobs."

Mack had read about the feud between the Police Department and the Mayor. He could hear the bitterness in the chief's voice. It wasn't his concern. The kid was.

The chief stood. He picked up the picture and handed it back to Mack. "Look Crawford, like I said, we'll take a shot at this, but you can understand how it is right now—a panic. Go ahead and fill out a report. We'll see what we can do about finding the kid."

Mack nodded, thanked the chief for his time, and walked out of the stuffy office. He sat down at a desk and completed the report handed to him by the desk sergeant. On television, the officers asked the questions, completed the paperwork themselves. *Maybe it's different in real life.* He glanced at the picture of the child wrapped in the fish net. Fear resided in those young eyes. He tossed the pen on the desk, stuffed the picture back in his pocket, and left the building. No one tried to stop him.

When he was a kid, he never thought about police work as being a job. Back then, in his mind, policemen and teachers lined up just below God. Of course, that was when he was a kid. They'd slipped a notch or two since then.

He didn't go back to work. Instead he picked up a six pack and went to his apartment, pacing the floor like an incarcerated panther. There was a little girl out there being exposed to a living hell. It couldn't be a family thing. He didn't believe that for a minute. He should have insisted the chief search the missing children reports—surely they had such a thing—but he was so stunned at their lack of interest, every logical thought went out of his head.

After a couple of beers and mulling things over, Mack decided to ask a few questions on his own. He wouldn't be able to sleep or focus on his job until he found her. The terror in her eyes screamed at him to do something. She couldn't be more than nine or ten. He wondered if she would ever smile again or if they'd already pushed her too far. He wondered if she was still alive. Time was of the essence. He could feel it.

He drove to the video store on the corner of Martial and Patout. They sold a large variety of magazines, from *Hotspot* to *Newsweek,* and rented the latest movie releases around-the-clock.

He entered through the glass door. The bell rang above his head.

Hank Breaux, the owner, was on his knees, shuffling magazines.

"How's it going, Hank?"

"I'm making a living, Crawford. That's about all I can say for it. What can I do for you?" He slashed stacks of bundled magazines as if racing the clock.

"I got a picture here I want you to look at. Tell me what you think."

"Let me see." Hank stuck out his beefy hand. "Cripes, what is this?" He handed it back quickly. "I don't deal with child porn; don't know anyone who does around here."

"Anybody ever come in looking for it? Do you carry any under the counter stuff at all?"

"A little S&M for special customers, but like I told you, I don't deal with child porn. It's sick."

"Anyone try to sell you any?"

Hank stood and stretched his back. "No. I'm one of two independent stores that isn't franchised. We're all going under. If you want my advice, I'd get rid of that picture and forget all about it."

Mack held it in front of Frank's face. "Look at her, Frank. Look at her face. Look at her eyes. What if she was your kid?"

Frank didn't answer.

"You have a night person?"

"Yeah, that would be Wanda. I'll talk to her and see if she knows anything. Someone may have tried to bootleg some of this junk in on her. Stop back by and I'll let you know."

Instead of returning to his empty apartment, Mack

68

went to the Boil Pit just a few blocks away. He had no desire to sit in his dreary garage apartment alone. Not tonight. He was jittery, up tight. Was it because of the picture, the lack of interest from law enforcement, or knowing his own child could very well be snatched off the school playground and put through the same kind of hell? Probably a combination of all those things.

He sat at the bar nursing a beer. The crowd was small; everyone seemed to know each other. He felt like odd man out, so he left.

Glancing at his watch, he figured Wanda might be behind the counter at the video store; he decided to swing by to talk with her. Sure, he trusted Frank to do it, but why wait?

Wanda was a busty, hard-looking woman. Hard to tell her age; her dyed black hair made her look forty-ish but for some reason Mack thought she could be younger. She eyed him warily. Or was it his imagination?

"I'm Mack Crawford. I was in here earlier talking to Hank."

"Yeah, he told me. I haven't seen any of that smut. Never had any request for it either." She pulled a dirty dust cloth from the back pocket of her stained, faded jeans and swiped at the counter.

"Just thought I'd check back by. If you remember anyone, give me a call. Frank has my number."

She didn't meet his eyes. "Will do, but no kiddy porn comes through here. And I don't expect it."

Mack went home. The night stretched longer than usual. He often suffered from insomnia, but tonight was worse. He got up, paced the floor, and watched the bayou meander behind his apartment. He couldn't get the little girl's face out of his mind. Was she asleep now? Having a nightmare? Crying for her mama and daddy? He didn't know whether to pray for her to be alive or pray that God had saved her by taking her home.

The next morning he was on the job an hour early, but no matter how hard he worked, he couldn't forget the kid. He couldn't concentrate.

By the time the five o'clock whistle blew, he was in his truck with a list of independent video stores. He figured the independent stores were the most likely to be involved in kiddie porn. According to his list, Primo Video, an adult store located on Interstate 10, was the only one open 24 hours a day specializing in free home delivery.

Free home delivery certainly lends itself to underground movies, he thought. He remembered when he was a kid, calling liquor stores that offered that kind of service. It didn't matter that he was underage. By the time the driver showed up with the bottle, all he was interested in was getting paid.

Primo Video was lit up like the Fourth of July. Mack pushed open the glass door that was covered with a life-size poster of Pamela Anderson. He wandered around, studying the DVDs shelved throughout the store, waiting for the little man behind the counter to be free of his customers.

When the man noticed him loitering, he asked, "You looking for something special, Mister?" The short red-haired guy held an unfiltered cigarette firmly between small dirty fingers.

Mack flashed the picture in front of his face. "You recognize this?"

The man barely looked at it. "Who are you? Law or her daddy?"

"Just a guy looking for answers. You see anything like this being passed around?"

"We don't deal in that stuff."

"Who does?"

Mack reached into his pocket and pulled out a twenty.

70

The clerk eyed the crisp green bill.

"Why don't you give me a soft drink and keep the change?" Mack suggested.

"Mister," the clerk whispered, "I'm a dead man if my boss finds out I talked to you. This ain't much of a job, but it's better than some I've had."

"Tell me what you know, and we've never met."

"My boss gives out a number for some flicks to special customers. I don't know what kind of flicks, just something we don't carry."

"Got the number?"

"It's in the office."

Mack waved the twenty, and the little man hurried out of the room.

He returned shortly, lighting another cigarette and walking a little taller than before.

"Here it is, and don't say where you got it."

Mack glanced at the slip of paper with numbers scrawled across it. He pulled out his cell and thumbed in the numbers.

"Acadian recreation. Please leave your name and number. We will return your call as soon as possible."

A recording. He looked up at the clerk who stared at him.

"How about the twenty?" the man asked.

Mack held the bill between two fingers. "What's your boss's name?"

He frowned, then rubbed the top of his red hair. "Clyde Dulie." He reached for the money.

Mack yanked it back. "Throw in a couple of Reese's Peanut Butter Cups with that soft drink."

Acadian Recreation was not listed in the phone directory. The operator couldn't help him either. Mack called again and left a fictitious name with his cell number. He wondered if they could detect the lie in his voice. Stretching out on the sofa, he stared absently at the sports page of the local newspaper.

Would they call back immediately or wait a day or two? Would they try to check him out?

Two hours later, he was dozing when his cell jarred him awake. He grabbed the phone. Acadian Recreation.

"Yeah."

"Bruce Waterman?" The woman used the fictitious name he'd left.

"Yeah," he said again.

"Who recommended you?"

"Clyde." He felt dirty repeating the name.

"What market?"

"Kid flicks. Something heavy."

The moment the words left his mouth, he knew he'd said too much. The dial tone echoed in his ear. She'd recognized his voice. That was okay. He'd recognized hers, too. *Wanda.* His whole body tightened. The pit of his stomach turned sour.

He pulled on a well-worn pair of lizards and buttoned his shirt. Was he close to finding the kid? Yeah, he could feel it in his gut.

Within moments he was in his pickup, heading to Hank's video store. There was a used car lot across the street and Mack turned into the alley behind it. He inched his truck in between the other vehicles and waited. Through the glass front, he observed Wanda moving around. He didn't like her, but something about her seemed vulnerable. He didn't understand it. He tried to listen to some music on the radio, but it agitated him instead of soothing him. His eyes never left Wanda. At four-forty-five a.m., he wandered over to the next door service station for a cup of coffee. Only a dozen customers had popped into the video store during the night. Surely Hank wasn't making enough to keep it open twenty-four hours a day—and pay Wanda.

Mack glanced at his watch. She'd get off soon, and

then she'd take him to the kid. He'd make sure of it. He wondered if he should call the police department, get some backup. With a snort, he decided against it. He didn't want to interfere with any job interviews they might have.

Mack dug his cell out of his pocket and called Garrett, his project manager. "I'll be late for work— in fact, I'll be very late." He didn't explain why and Garrett didn't ask. Mack crammed the cell back in his pocket and looked up just as Wanda's relief entered the store.

What did he think he was doing? He was taking the law into his own hands. He had no business in this. He might get himself killed or worse, get the kid killed—if she was still alive. His heart beat rapidly. Perspiration broke out on his forehead and just above his upper lip.

Wanda came out of the store and got into a battered Monte Carlo. The hubcaps were missing and one of the taillights was out. The thing made enough noise to wake the whole town. He pulled his truck slowly out of the used car lot and followed.

Wanda drove down Patout which took them to Main Street right through the center of the still sleeping little town. She took a left. Soon, the city lights were behind them and Mack knew Wanda was headed for the Atchafalaya Swamp. The road became a narrow two-lane. Mack wished he was more familiar with the territory. The Atchafalaya Swamp could be bad.

Wanda picked up speed. She must have spotted him. They were making the curves a little faster than Mack cared to. After glancing down at his speedometer, he looked up and saw nothing ahead of him. She must've turned off just around the last curve. He slammed on his brakes, looked in the rearview mirror just as Wanda reappeared. She pulled up behind him

73

and got out of her car, angrily. The woman had guts. Confrontational type.

"What do you think you're doing, you sorry Texas son of a—"

Mack jumped out of his truck, running toward her. He saw fear in her eyes. He liked it. He wanted to scare her to death. No, he wanted more than that; he wanted to beat her to death, but not before he found the little girl.

"Where is she?" he demanded. "Where's the girl?" She tried to run. He grabbed her arm and twisted it.

"Hey, what the—"

"Tell me where the kid is or I'll break it for you." He wasn't in the habit of threatening or harming women. He kept the missing child at the front of his mind. "For the kid," he added.

Wanda grunted, kicked at his groin but missed. Mack slammed her against the car.

"Anytime you're ready to talk, I'm listening," he whispered in her ear. She smelled. He drew back.

She began to cry, loud sobs. "I hate you. I hate all men who think they can—"

He gave her arm another little twist. He was surprised at the rage he felt. He'd never hit a woman. It wasn't his nature to lose his temper with the opposite sex. If it wasn't for the picture of the kid—the terror in her eyes, and what his imagination was doing to him, he wouldn't be so tempted now.

"Is she still alive?" he asked, trying to calm himself.

"Of course she's still alive. He won't hurt her. She's his little girl."

Her words chilled him to the bone. "Where is she? Take me to her."

"She's at the camp." She tried to get away from him but Mack held her tight. One arm was twisted behind her back, and he held a handful of her coarse black hair. It felt dirty, oily in his hand.

74

"I can't take you there. He'll kill me."

"We'll have to take that chance. You got a gun?" He asked opening the car door.

"No," she answered.

Mack reached his hand beneath the seat of her car and pulled out a sawed off shotgun. "I'm sure I misunderstood you." He pointed it at her. "Now move toward the truck."

He drove with the shotgun in his left hand aimed at Wanda. She gave him directions—cursed him, pleaded, sobbed.

"You don't know the hell I go through. Being the bread-winner and making a little of nothing. I had to marry him. I had to do what he said."

She wasn't making any sense. "Where'd you get the kid?" Mack asked.

"Kids ain't hard to find. They run around everywhere."

"You didn't answer the question."

"New Orleans. Picked her up in Jackson Square during the tail end of Mardi Gras. Lots of kids around—everywhere," she repeated.

She mumbled directions. He followed them, warning her that she'd better be telling him the truth. Eventually they turned onto shale which suddenly changed to nothing more than a dirt path.

"We have to leave the truck here. Cross over in the boat," Wanda said.

Mack felt jittery, as if he was walking into an ambush, but there was no turning back now. He wished he could recall what to do from some of the war movies he'd seen, some of the westerns. Dirty Harry flashed into his head. He definitely couldn't claim experience in this line of work.

The crack of dawn was slipping up on them; the swamp was a mass of grayness. A thick mist rose from the water. Mack sniffed, filling his nostrils with the musky smell of vegetation. The moss hanging from the trees look like miniature bodies in the dimness of dawn. He shuddered.

They walked through the wet, knee-high grass toward the water until they came to the boat. Once seated, Wanda pulled at the throttle. The motor started on the third attempt, a loud intrusion in the stillness of the swamp. She guided the boat through the water lilies, clearly knowing the way. Mack looked out across the bayou, then down at his boots. He pulled them off, remembering an uncle who drowned with his boots on. He might get killed trying to save a little girl from living hell, but he wasn't about to fall into a Louisiana bayou and drown because he had his boots on.

Wanda cut the motor and began to paddle towards a small island. The fog hung heavy across the basin. Several fishermen on their way to a favorite spot, waved at them, totally unaware of what was about to go down.

"We've lived at the camp ever since Boogie got laid off at the plant. Lost the house to Katrina. Couldn't find no work nowhere. When his buddies started their movie business, they approached me since I work at the video store. You making a big mistake, Mister. She ain't part of the movies. He's good to the kid just like he was good to me."

"Yeah, right."

"I ain't kidding. He never hurt her. Just wanted her 'cause she looked like his little girl."

"Then why the picture?"

Wanda hesitated. "It was me. I'm the one who took the picture and left it on the bank."

Mack shot her a glance, wondered if she was telling the truth. He decided it didn't matter.

"You can tell it to the cops when this is all over."

"He'll fight you for her. People get killed in these

swamps all the time and nobody ever knows it. Easiest place in the world to kill a man and get rid of the remains. You could end up alligator food."

"Shut up." He didn't want to hear it. As useless as they may have seemed, maybe he should have called the cops. He should have been as methodical as he was at work instead of letting his emotions drive him to search for the child. He should have made a plan. Too late now. He'd have to go with the flow. But keep his wits about him.

"Who's with him—anyone?"

"Don't know. Maybe just the kid. Maybe his friends that live a mile or so down the way. They're helping him build up the pier."

"If you set me up, lady, this shotgun is going off in the back of your head."

"I won't do nothing."

Reaching the island, Mack tugged on his boots. They got out of the boat, edging it up to the land. Wanda led the way, walking slowly through the brush.

They approached the cabin from the rear. A 55 gallon drum piled high with trash reeked of crawfish shells and who knew what else. The leaning outdoor toilet with the lopsided door proved the builder was no carpenter. A sickening odor emanated from it and joined forces with the garbage, permeating the air. Mack wanted to gag but focused his mind on the task at hand. He had to find the child and get her out of this dump.

They crept slowly around the side of the dilapidated house, staying in the brush, then worked their way to the front, stepping into the water. Mack tripped on a cypress knee. He cursed, held the gun high so it wouldn't get wet. Tried to control the panic that rose to his throat.

"Don't try anything, lady. I'm wound tight," he warned and pressed the barrell of the gun to the back of her head.

They waited, watched the old shack for any kind of movement. Boogie must not have heard the splash.

"Call for him," Mack whispered. "Tell him you need some help with the groceries."

"He wouldn't believe that. I never ask him for help with that kinda stuff."

Frustrated, Mack eased out of the swamp, pulling Wanda close. They made their way up the shallow embankment and over to a large Cypress tree. He shoved her against its trunk. "Stay here. Make no sound," he ordered, poking the shotgun in her face. "You understand me?"

She nodded.

There was a small garden between the house and the water. He was beside it, working his way toward the shack when he heard a door creak open. Boogie came flying out, his rifle waist-high. He was shirtless and his filthy pants hung low on his hips, exposing his navel. He pulled the trigger, not bothering to aim.

Mack hit the ground. He got to one knee, pulled the sawed-off shotgun tight to his shoulder and fired.

His arms flew up above his head and he fell backwards. Stunned, he scrambled for cover, half-expecting others to pile out the door. No one came. His shoulder felt as though it had been dislocated. He looked around and saw the body.

Inching his way toward the blood-spattered man on the ground, Mack almost gagged at the sight of the empty chest cavity. He felt for a pulse, knowing it was just an act of humanity. The man was dead.

He moved cautiously to the house, stepped up on the make-shift porch, and looked through the door. He felt a noise come from his throat and wondered if he was going to get hysterical. The one room shack was filthy and cluttered. A soiled mattress lay on the floor and backless chairs surrounded a table piled high with empty beer bottles. But where was the girl? For a moment he wondered if it had been a mistake. Had he killed a man unnecessarily?

"Anyone here?" His voice sounded scratchy. "Hey kid, where are you?"

A sound came from the closet. He heard soft weeping. He rushed over and yanked open the door. The child stood against the wall, huddled in the corner of the empty closet, dressed in nothing but a man's dirty shirt. She drew back in horror. She didn't look like her picture. She was thinner, her hair longer and matted together with dirt and sweat. She was filthy, smelled sour.

"It's okay," he whispered. "I'm here to help you. Everything is going to be okay." He held out his hand, but she didn't take it and huddled tighter against the wall. "I promise I'm going to take you home. Home to your family, your mama and daddy," he explained, softly. "I promise."

The little girl sobbed loudly, falling to the floor.

"Will you take me home to my mama and daddy, too?"

He turned. Wanda stood in the door. Tears ran down her cheeks. "He took me when I was nine," she whispered.

The morning sun was too bright. Only moments earlier it had been dawn. Everything seemed to be moving at double pace, like an old movie. Boogie's blood was redder than Mack thought it should be. The three of them stood on the porch. The little girl held his hand tightly.

"Don't be afraid," Mack said when he saw her look over at Boogie's body.

She broke away from him, running over to the lifeless form. For one horrible moment, Mack thought she was going to throw herself down beside him, mourn him. She didn't. She kicked him. She kicked and screamed over and over again while tears flowed down her sweet dirty face.

Mack pulled her away. She clung to his legs and sobbed. Wanda did her own share of sobbing.

"It's okay. Everything's going to be okay." But he knew it wasn't true. Not for either of them. Wanda had lost a lifetime with her family.

And this baby girl—who knows what she'd experienced? She'd been so terrified she'd probably prayed for death.

"From here on out, everything is going to be okay," he whispered again, fighting the tears that came to his own eyes. "No one…nothing will ever hurt you again."

The End

Jessica Ferguson is a staff writer for Southern Writers Magazine and the author of several novels and novellas—both published and unpublished. She fantasizes that one day she'll wake up and all those manuscripts on her hard drive will be, miraculously, revised and edited. In her spare time, Jess enjoys Bible Studies, bean bag baseball, breakfast/brainstorming with friends and playing with her recently retired husband.
www.jessicafergusonwriter.com
www.facebook.com/jessica.ferguson.3557
www.pinterest.com/jessyferguson

Cypress, Like the Tree
By Yolanda Renée

I boarded the bus and relief surged through me. Finally, with the decision made, the horror was over. It wasn't the way I'd intended to travel, but things came to a head way too soon, and a bus ticket was all I could afford. I settled near the back and hoped a sweet older woman would sit beside me. Instead, two policemen boarded. After looking over all the passengers, they made their way to my seat.

"Mrs. Allan? Mrs. William Allan?" one officer said.

I sat up. "Yes," I muttered. "I'm Mrs. Allan."

"Please come with us, ma'am," the man said and motioned for me to stand.

"Why? What's this about?"

The men let me enter the aisle. Then one of them grabbed my arms and brutally handcuffed me.

"Mrs. Allan, you're under arrest for the murder of your husband."

"Murder?"

The other passengers murmured as they marched me off the bus.

"Bill's dead?" The world went black. When I came to, I was lying on the backseat of a patrol car. I managed to sit up.

"I told you she was fine," the officer driving said to his partner.

"Is my husband really dead?"

"Like you didn't know," he chortled, then he began spouting my Miranda rights. I heard the words, "You have the right to remain silent," and decided it was my best bet. But the tears fell. At first, I wasn't sure if I was mourning Bill or my own predicament. That

81

bastard had been abusing me since the day after we said our vows just fifteen months earlier, but I'd never wished him dead. Now, he was, and somehow, they'd judged me guilty.

Bill cheated on me with my bridesmaid a day after our wedding, and at the NCO club, he had a posse of women. Murder made perfect sense, but what made them suspect me?

They held me in a dirty gray box of a room designed to turn the most minimal claustrophobic into a raging maniac. A camera recorded all from the far corner, and a grungy mirror or one-way window mocked me from across the small room. I felt exposed, constrained, and I sensed the walls closing in. Were they watching? I knew they were using silence and time against me.

I bowed my head over my arms and cried, thought about the dilemma I was in, and then cried some more. After drenching my sleeves with tears and snot, I sat up and corralled my emotions. After two hours, the same policemen walked into the room and removed the handcuffs.

I rubbed my sore wrists and glared with defiance at my jailers. Silence, my ally.

A detective entered the room. His superior than thou aura wafted off him like cheap aftershave and I knew he was a detective before he even opened his mouth. Tall, thin, and rumpled, he reminded me of an anorexic Clark Kent. Was this Superman in disguise?

"Mrs. Allan, please accept my apology. These two were told to bring you in for questioning. Not make an arrest. Somewhere the message got scrambled." He scowled at the two men. "You're dismissed gentlemen but first bring the lady a cup of coffee." He offered his hand. "I'm Detective Cypress, like the tree."

I took his hand. "I'm not under arrest?" He shook his head. I dropped his soft flesh. He was no Ironman.

"May I have tea instead of coffee?"

"Of course," he said, nodding a *fetch it* signal to a new man who'd just stepped into the room. His partner, I assumed.

I walked to the mirror and wiped the tears and mascara from my face with my sleeve. The detective offered me his hanky.

"No, thank you." I turned to face him. "Tell me about my husband."

"Please sit." He held out a chair.

"I prefer to stand."

He sighed. "Fine. Your husband's body was found on Red Clay Road a few hours ago. Deep in the brush."

"Why do you think I killed him?"

He cleared his throat. "Like I said, a mistake was made. Can you tell me where you were this morning?"

"I was with John Clément. After Bill left for work, John helped me pack my belongings, and drove me to the bus station."

"That's what he claimed. Why were you with Mr. Clément?"

"I assume you already know that answer."

"I'd like your version."

I hated his smugness. "And you also like to have the answers before you ask the questions."

He shrugged.

"Bill and I had a fight last night."

"What about?"

"Laundry. Everything was dirty. I wanted to go to the laundromat. Bill didn't want me to leave."

"What happened?"

"He wouldn't listen to reason. I was starting a new job this morning. I needed clean clothes."

"And?" the detective probed.

"I wouldn't give up the car keys so Bill went outside to disable the car, and I locked the door behind him. It infuriated him. He screamed and pounded so fiercely I was afraid he'd tear the door off its hinges. I unlocked it, but he slapped me so hard I saw stars." I touched my cheek. "His fingerprints ...." I lowered my head, letting my hair cover the evidence. My face flushed.

Cypress lifted my chin toward the light, pushed my hair aside. "That must've hurt."

I scrutinized him through my lashes. Does he *care*? I crossed the room, stared into the mirror, and wondered how many men were standing on the other side. I turned my back to them. Do men even know the meaning of the word *care*?

His partner returned with tea in a Styrofoam cup and a box of tissues. He put them on the table, whispered something in the detective's ear, and left the room.

"Then what happened?" the detective asked and straddled a chair. With his hands behind his head, he leaned back and watched me. I had my answer.

"I ran out of the house. John was on his porch. He'd heard the commotion. He seemed concerned."

"Why didn't you go to your friend Madura's place?"

"She has a small daughter, and if Bill followed me, I couldn't risk bringing that kind of horror to a friend's doorstep. Besides, I knew how much her husband hated Bill."

I cringed and closed my eyes. *Oh God, did I just implicate my only friend's husband?* "I mean he hated the way Bill treated me. At least that's what Madura said. I've never really spoken to Gary about it. I only spent time with Madura."

"I see," the detective said thoughtfully. "What about Bruce Smith? He was home."

"He's a small man. He could never have stood up to Bill." I sat down across from the detective.

"But John could?"

"I thought so. John is larger and older than Bill, and I assumed.... Well, I just thought he was the best choice at that moment."

"What about your landlady, Mrs. Johnson? Was she home?"

"I think so. Her lights were on, but Anna has two small kids, and I couldn't take that chance. Besides, I needed help, someone Bill couldn't intimidate."

"I can see that. Had Bill been violent before?"

I laughed. Actually laughed, then I swallowed several mouthfuls of the now cold tea and gathered myself. "Sorry, your question just struck me odd. I'm afraid my emotions are raw." I ripped several tissues from the box, covered my face, and sobbed. "I still can't believe he's gone." I looked around the room. "Or that I'm here. He was abusive, but..."

"More tea?" the detective offered as he sat up straighter in his chair.

I shook my head, blew my nose, and answered his question. "The abuse began shortly after we were married. I never ever got a hint of it when we were dating. Now, looking back, I realize that I should've recognized the signs."

"What signs?"

"The way he treated his mother. She went after him with a broom handle once, and he turned it around on her. I should've known then. Yes, in answer to your question, Bill mocked, downgraded, hit, shoved, and once choked me to unconsciousness. It was that incident that convinced me I had to leave."

"Why didn't you?"

"Bill controlled the purse strings. I hoped to make enough money with this new job so I could disappear. Madura warned me. She told me tragedy always follows violence. She offered to loan me the funds, but I thought I could do it on my own. I just needed to keep from riling Bill. I failed."

"After you went to Mr. Clément's place, what happened?"

"John gave me a glass of whiskey and a cup of tea. I was near hysterical. Then I saw Bill coming across the park and panicked. John told me to sit still and went outside. He and Bill argued, but John managed to calm him down because Bill went back to our trailer."

"What happened next?" The detective was calm, methodical, and I had a feeling every word I said was being recorded and that every gesture was or would be studied.

"We talked. John convinced me it was time to leave my husband, money or no money. He offered to buy me a plane ticket, but I told him I had enough to take a bus home."

"Where's home?"

"New York."

"You spent the night with John?"

"Yes, on his couch. He works the night shift. When he returned in the morning, well, you know the rest."

"What time did your husband leave?"

"Six. Bill takes his motorcycle so I can use the car to get to work or run errands.

"If the car was there, why didn't you use it to drive home this morning?"

"I assumed it was still disabled. Besides, it's Bill's car. I packed my things and left the car keys on the table."

"But first, you went to the laundromat. That seems like an odd move. I thought you were concerned about getting away from your abusive husband."

I nodded, pursed my lips, and pulled my hair back into a ponytail to cool my neck. The atmosphere felt stifling. "Packing dirty clothes just felt wrong. Besides, Bill was at work, and I had time to kill. Sorry, I didn't mean..." I covered my face with my hands.

I sighed. "Poor choice of words. What I mean is the bus didn't leave until eleven, and I felt safe with

John. You haven't said, Detective. How did Bill die?"

"The coroner's report isn't in yet."

"I guess being run off the road would make for multiple wounds. I hope he didn't suffer."

"That's magnanimous."

"Not really. Bill was only abusive when he was drunk or angry. Most of the time he was an overgrown kid in search of love. I'll never forget the day the neighborhood kids knocked on the door and asked if Billy could come out and play."

"So the marriage wasn't all bad?"

"It had its moments. In spite of the other women, the alcohol, and the beatings, Bill could be a regular person." I smiled. "I think I'll hold on to those in-between moments." I wiped at more tears, stood, and stretched. "May I leave now?"

"Yes, of course. I'll drive you home."

Home. The thought that I still had one hadn't hit me. "I guess. I have a few details to take care of before I leave, don't I?"

"Until we've solved this case, you'll have to stay put."

"Oh," was the only word I could form. My mouth was suddenly dry. I wasn't under arrest, but I was a suspect. My heart raced, my face flushed, and silent prayers streamed through my head.

He opened the door and maneuvered me through the station past a sea of staring faces. Before we left his partner handed over my thoroughly ransacked purse and suitcase.

In the car, Cypress asked a few inconsequential questions, which I answered, but mostly I stared out the window. My life had changed, but I had no idea how much at that moment.

Before we arrived at the trailer, he told me that Bill had disabled the carburetor, but the car was drivable now. I thanked him and said goodbye. Then I stepped inside the trailer. The place had been searched. Fingerprint dust covered everything. Yet, in the midst of the chaos, our wedding bands, something Bill never wore, still sat on the mantel in front of our wedding photo.

I shook my head as I looked at the faces smiling back at me from the picture. How foolish we were. Two people couldn't have been more unsuited for one another. Now the groom was dead and the bride the top suspect. I made the sign of the cross. Heaven help me.

A knock sounded on the door. I didn't want or need company, but I answered it.

"John." He looked a wreck, sweat dripped from his face, and deep lines creased his forehead. "Are you all right?"

"That's my question. You were at the station for a long time."

"Were you there?"

"Yes, but they didn't keep me long."

"I'm sorry, John. I'd invite you in, but I was just going to lie down. I'm exhausted."

"No, that's all right. I have to get some sleep, too. I just wanted to make sure you were okay. Hearing how Bill was shot, I wanted you to know that you're safe, Bruce and I will keep watch."

"Thank you." I touched his arm. "Especially for your help last night, this morning, and now. I just hope they find Bill's—" I stopped speaking, and my hand went to my heart. "You said Bill was shot!"

"Yes, didn't they tell you how he died?"

"No. I just assumed someone ran him off the road." I rubbed my throbbing forehead. "I'm their *top* suspect. They didn't tell me because they hoped I'd slip up. Sorry, John. This nightmare is giving me a headache, can we talk later?"

"Don't you worry, no nightmare can last forever.

You'll see. It'll be over soon!"

I sighed. "From your mouth to Gods' ears."

He gave me a halfhearted salute. "Get some sleep."

* * *

Amazingly, I slept well and awoke around six P.M. Exactly twelve hours had passed since Bill died, some of the longest hours in my life. I dressed and opened a can of vegetable soup. I'd only eaten a few bites when another knock sounded.

The way Detective Cypress pushed his way in, I knew it wasn't going to be a pleasant visit.

"I hope you've gotten some rest, Mrs. Allan, because I have a few more questions. You don't mind, do you?" He walked straight to the wedding photo.

"No, Detective. I don't mind. Please, have a seat."

"You never framed your wedding photo. Why?" He picked up the cheap cardboard frame that had come from the photographer, but he was watching me.

I shrugged. "We live in a trailer, Detective. Money doesn't stretch far."

He pursed his lips. "Looks like an extravagant wedding."

"His mother's idea. She paid for and planned it, I just showed up."

He put the picture back. "Interesting."

"How do you mean?"

"He mistreated her, and yet, she spent that kind of money?"

"An only son. An odd relationship." I wasn't sure what he was getting at. It was unnerving. "I'm thirsty." I headed to the kitchen. "Would you care for a drink? I have Jack Daniels, iced tea, and instant coffee."

"I'd love Jack on ice."

Interesting, a cop who drinks on the job. I carried my glass of tea and his whiskey into the living room. He downed his drink in one gulp.

"Tell me, Mrs. Allan, with all these men falling at

your feet, which one did you beguile into killing your husband?"

I could tell by his tone he was trying to rile me, and he'd gone for the throat. I frowned, and my stomach churned. "I'm sorry, Detective, what men?" I settled on the arm of the easy chair.

"Well, for starters, there's Madura's husband, Gary, John, the rescuer, and Bruce, the little guy. Then there's the handyman, Trent, and several of the guards on the chain gang. Apparently, they know you from your solo bike rides on Red Clay Road. Were you searching for the perfect spot to murder your husband?"

"Whoa, Detective, I can only handle one outrageous accusation at a time. Slow down, or I might get flustered and confess."

He leaned close as though I'd do just that.

"The only men I've even spoken to, and never more than a quick hello, are my direct neighbors." I settled into the chair and folded my legs under me. "I've never said one word to those other men."

"Oh, come on. A pretty little thing like you? A tilt of the head is considered flirting."

"Detective, I was faithful to my husband, my very jealous husband. Why the third degree? What's really going on? John told me Bill was shot to death. Why did you let me believe he'd been run off the road?"

"I don't volunteer information. I'm the one gathering it. But I find it interesting that you've already spoken to John."

"He came to the door right after I got home. Which, if you're the cop I think you are, you already knew that before you arrived."

He looked at me carefully. I stirred the ice in my tea with my finger.

"Then tell me, Mata Hari." He leaned even closer. "If you didn't convince one of these men to kill the bastard, which one do you think did it?"

I sucked the wetness from my finger, brought the glass to my lips, and gazed into his dark brown eyes. I couldn't believe what he was saying, and yet.... I shook my head dismissively. "No, that doesn't make any sense. Why would any of those men kill Bill? They don't even know me."

He sat back in his chair. "Maybe they do. Maybe they don't. But I'd bet my last dollar it's one of them. That is if it isn't you." He stood. "Whether you did it, or one of your admirers did it for you, I promise I will get to the bottom of it."

"You're wrong." I faced him. "You're wrong about me, and them. Have you investigated his girlfriends? Maybe there's a jealous husband or boyfriend."

"We're checking, but I've talked to all these men, and they all said your husband deserved to die."

On his way out, Detective Nasty fired his parting shot. "In their words, there's motive. You've bewitched these men. I've seen it dozens of times. Evil, Mrs. Allan. Or should I call you *Lillian*? Your name fits. Pure evil."

"Lilith is the evil one, not *Lillian.*"

He just smiled. Then he was gone, but the implication hung in the air like pungent smoke. He characterized me as a harpy, a succubus, a woman so evil she could make men commit murder with a snap of her fingers. My heart beat erratically, my stomach clenched, and I swore I felt Bill's cold dead hands around my throat.

Shivering with fear and disbelief, I picked up our wedding photo and tore it into pieces. I threw it, and the rings, into the garbage.

* * *

The next morning, while ignoring the eggs and toast I'd prepared for breakfast, I reviewed the day before. Timing. The answer to Bill's death was all in the timing. I knew where I was when he died, but where were the others? I had to know for sure, especially the men the detective mentioned. Did they know something I didn't?

I almost laughed as I got onto my bicycle. Playing detective wasn't my forte, but I couldn't just let them hang me. The handyman, Trent, was working on a trailer across the road. I stopped to speak to him first.

"Detective Cypress said he spoke to you about my husband. Did you see something or someone who might've done this?"

"Oh no ma'am, but I sure saw and heard the way he treated you." He smiled and yellow teeth stained with chew churned my empty stomach. He removed his hat and wiped his forehead with a dirty bandana. "No woman should be manhandled like that. I'm sorry for what you've suffered."

He sounded sincere, but his words made my creep factor meter go ballistic. Now I was positive he was the peeping Tom I'd seen looking in our windows a few weeks back. That made him a creepy busybody, but I didn't think he had the backbone to kill anybody.

"Thank you. I appreciate that. Have a good day." I quickly took off.

I followed Red Clay Road toward the base, but I wasn't sure why. Bill died there. Did I really want to visit the site? I was about to turn around when I spotted the chain gang. I wondered which of them had spoken to the detective. Normally, I kept my head down when I rode past them. I had no idea what any of them could've said. Maybe none of them had said anything. The police are known to pad the truth. Perhaps that's all this was, a lie cooked up to unnerve their chief suspect. With a final glance, I turned around and pedaled in the other direction. The trip was fruitless. I'm not a sleuth, but at least the long ride cleared my head.

When I arrived home an hour later, the detective was waiting.

"Good afternoon, Lillian," he said.

"It's Mrs. Allan to you, Detective."

"Yes, of course," he said with a tip of his hat and a sick grin.

I parked my bike, and he followed me into the house. After mopping the sweat from my face, I grabbed a bottle of water from the fridge and downed it. "Can you make this quick? I need a shower."

"Actually, I have a timeline. I'd like to go over the details with you."

"Fine, but a shower first. Be back in fifteen minutes." Without waiting for his answer, I headed for the bathroom.

As I shampooed my hair, I thought about Bill and all the people with a reason to kill him. Sure, I had a motive, but so did half the state of Georgia. Hopefully, the timeline would help them narrow the field.

I returned to the kitchen to find that the Detective had poured two glasses of iced tea. "I thought you might like something cold." He pointed to a chair.

I sat.

He dropped a yellow pad and pen on the table.

"So, how can I help?"

"You said you saw Bill leave on his motorcycle around 6 A.M. Is that right?"

"Yes, that was his usual time. He started work at seven, but he always ate breakfast with his buddies first."

"The coroner put his death between six and seven, so that works out. Describe exactly what you were doing and what you saw."

"I was making a cup of tea in John's kitchen. His picture window faces this direction, but I was working at the sink and only glanced this way when I heard Bill's motorcycle engine turn over. I saw him drive

CYPRESS, LIKE THE TREE

out."

"What was he wearing?"

"His uniform, and over that, his black leather jacket and helmet. What he always wore."

"I see." Cypress made notes. "Good. Thank you."

"Have you found anyone else who saw Bill leave that morning?" I asked.

"Yes, several people. They confirmed he left at his usual time."

"Then what's the problem?"

"You're lying."

"No!" I hit the table with my fist. "John's clock chimed the hour and John came through the door just as Bill pulled out. We commented on his departure because it meant I could get back into the house to pack."

"John confirmed that. But someone's lying, and since we have a witness that saw John arrive home at 6:30 you're the liar. Admit it. You killed your husband. You and you alone had motive and opportunity. Confess. It'll go easier on you. Being abused the way you were."

"No!" I stood. "You're wrong. I didn't kill my husband!"

Cypress stood, too. "Then who did?"

"I have no idea. A jealous husband? Somebody with a grudge? I just know it wasn't me. I'd finally decided to leave him."

The detective shook his head, spun me around, and had me handcuffed before I could think. We were at the front door and down the steps of the porch before I could catch my breath.

Typical, my only defense–tears. The neighbors had gathered to see the widow arrested for the murder of her military husband. I barely held onto my sanity as we walked to the car. I foolishly prayed for invisibility. Then I noticed the silence. Had I gone deaf, had the world? I should have prayed for deliverance. Unfortunately, neither was forthcoming.

* * *

Abandoned in the same dirty gray box, I waited and waited. Again, I sat alone, and again, time was on their side. Not mine.

Two hours later, they moved me to another room. It was brighter, had a round table with padded chairs, and a credenza with coffee and tea in the corner. They removed my handcuffs and let me fix a cup of tea. Had they changed their minds again? I knew they were watching. I worried about what would come next, but I didn't have to wait for long because an officer led Bruce into the room. His eyes were red...puffy?

"Bruce, are you all right?"

"I'm fine. I hope you don't mind. They said you haven't called an attorney, so they're letting me act as consultant. I have a list of the good ones. You just tell me who you prefer and I'm on it."

I was shocked by his presence. Other than a wave or nod of hello in the trailer park, we'd never spoken before. What were the police hoping to learn from him? "Thank you, but I don't have a clue. If you've done the research, please decide for me. But, I don't have any money. I can't afford an attorney."

"Don't you worry. We'll raise the money. Or, he'll do it *pro bono*."

"You don't think I'm guilty?"

He put his hand over mine. "Heavens, no. No one does. You just have to stay strong."

I wiped at my tears. "So much easier said than done."

The door opened and Bruce got up to leave. "I'll be in touch. If not me, your attorney. Stay strong, Lillian. We believe in you."

I smiled, but the moment the door closed, hope deserted me, and the walls started closing in again.

Then John walked in.

Sobbing, I hurried to the safety of his arms. "I'm sorry, John. I'm a wreck." I covered my face. "I don't know what to do."

"Don't you dare apologize. This has been one hell of a few days for you, but don't you worry. We'll see you through this. Whatever the bail is, we'll raise it. I promise. Just don't speak to anyone. Wait for your lawyer."

"I will. Thank you."

They only gave us five minutes, and I was alone, again, lost and alone. Bill was gone, but his cruelty had taken a different manifestation.

* * *

Bail was denied, but my attorney promised an acquittal. There were only two good things about being locked up. I lost weight, and my friends didn't fail me.

At the trial, the prosecutor made his case. "The State will prove that this young woman had motive, opportunity, and she found the means to take the life of this brave airman, William Allan. After a violent argument with her husband, she went to John Clément's place for help. A neighbor who comforted her, and allowed her to spend the night while he went to work.

"Instead of using this time to cool off, Lillian Allan planned and then carried out the cold-blooded murder of her husband. She found John Clément's handgun, then waited on Red Clay Road for her husband's appearance. Did Lillian Allan convince him that she wanted to make up? We'll probably never know, but she waited until he turned away and then shot him in the back of the head. Lillian Allan is a cold-blooded killer. Leaving wasn't good enough, she had to destroy her husband."

On the stand, John swore his gun was taken

months earlier, but he'd never reported it missing. The jury didn't believe him. I saw the frowns, the shaking heads, but it was the looks they shot my way that made my toes curl.

This horrid man in a well-tailored suit went on to say I'd hurried back to John's trailer, where I played a recorded sound of a motorcycle for him when he walked in the door. The only reason the clock chimed six, he said, was because I'd changed the setting.

With Bruce on the stand, my attorney forced him to admit under oath that he was infatuated with me. He did the same with John, but John would only agree to loving me as a father would love a daughter. However, both men revealed in their own words, that because of the way Bill treated me, they believed he deserved what he got and were surprised someone hadn't killed him sooner.

John testified that he'd heard and seen Bill leaving for work, but the prosecutor insisted that I'd tricked him by setting the clock back. John was steadfast, but the jury saw John as a lovesick fool.

John also confessed to giving me several glasses of whiskey that evening to calm my nerves. And that yes, although he'd left me alone in his trailer, he'd also communicated frequently with Bruce, who checked on me several times during the night. Both John and Bruce said I was so out of it, I had no idea anyone else was there.

Because of those admissions, my attorney insisted it was Bruce and John's idea to kill Bill. He said between them, and entirely without my knowledge, they'd pulled it off.

During closing arguments, he spelled it out in detail. "Gentlemen of the jury, this innocent woman has hurt no one, but she was beaten, cheated on, and her life was threatened daily. She finally found the courage to leave her cruel husband, but he wasn't about to let her go."

He reminded the jury of Bill's words to John the night he met him in the middle of the trailer court after our fight. "Bill Allan told John Clément that she would never get away from him. She belonged to him, and that it'd be over his dead body that another man would ever claim her. Having witnessed his escalating violence toward her for fifteen months, Bruce Smith and John Clément knew William Allan spoke the truth."

"Outraged, these two men took the situation in hand. They waited for Bill to leave for work, disabled him, and put him in Bruce's car. Bruce put Allan's leather jacket on, and John went to his trailer to rouse Lillian so she could witness her husband leave for work. Except it wasn't William Allan, it was Bruce Smith on that motorcycle. Bruce took the cycle to the murder site and then hoofed it back to the trailer park where he met up with John.

"At this time Lillian was back in her own trailer, packing. John and Bruce then delivered an unconscious Allan to the murder site on Red Clay Road and killed him. But they'd almost forgotten the leather jacket. It was put on the body after the kill shot. That ladies and gentleman is why there was no blood on the coat. Gentlemen of the jury, Lillian Allan is innocent!"

Was the jury buying it? I found hope.

My attorney was worth his fee. He'd created reasonable doubt.

It also didn't hurt that my attorney got Detective Cypress to admit that there were other suspects with stronger motives, but getting the chief detective to admit he had doubts about my guilt made the biggest impression. Without the gun, their evidence was all circumstantial.

It worked. I was acquitted.

Bruce and John came under scrutiny, but neither broke, and they both passed a lie detector test. After all, they'd done nothing wrong.

* * *

The sun was high, the waves hypnotizing, and my bank account full. Bill had several life insurance policies. A lovely surprise, and one I'm taking advantage of.

"Well, Lilith, I mean Lillian, are you enjoying your freedom?"

I looked into the dark eyes of Detective Cypress.

"Bermuda seems to agree with you. I don't see any black and blue marks. Have you chosen a less violent paramour this time?"

I looked out over the ocean. What do you say to a man like Cypress? A man who looks at you and knows your deepest, darkest secret?

"What are you doing here, Detective Tree, I mean Cypress? Isn't there another innocent suspect to hound?" I smiled, but I could barely keep from laughing. His alabaster body, while a solid nine, reflected the sun.

"I've missed your sense of humor." He sat down in the chair beside me. "Ah, this is the life, isn't it?"

"Uh huh." I laid back in the chair.

"You know the smartest thing you did was to have Bill take off his jacket. Great red herring. The removal would only make sense if someone meant to use it to impersonate him.

I didn't say a word. The detective wanted to talk, I'd let him. That silence thing still worked for me.

"We had it right. I just wish I knew how you convinced John and Bruce to lie for you. Or where you hid the gun. Come on fess up. No one can do anything about it now."

I sipped my Long Island Iced Tea, ignoring his plea. Although the timeline was tricky, I knew I'd get back to the trailer before John. After all, he'd promised to get my favorite green tea and chocolate croissants from Starbucks. And surprisingly it takes no time to kill a person. As for the gun, I threw it down one of the many snake burros in the brush along Red Clay Road.

"Would you like to use my sunscreen? That delicate skin of yours will burn quickly," I offered.

"I've got it covered. I'd just like to know; did you convince Bill that a quickie before work would heal all wounds?"

I drank the rest of my tea and continued to gaze at the waves. Yes, Detective Cypress knew all my secrets. Bill stopped the moment he saw me on the road. Makeup sex, something Bill thought could absolve him, undid him.

Still, it was pure luck that no one saw a hooded rider cutting through the brush at dawn and skirting between the trailers of the park on an old bike with bald tires. However, I will never understand how Bruce or John could allow themselves to be considered suspects– for me.

Although, who could blame a middle-aged man for being distracted, especially when a certain naked, nubile nineteen-year-old stepped into the room combing her hair dry after a shower? After all, I had to wash off that nasty gunshot residue, didn't I?

"Double jeopardy," the detective repeated. "You can't be tried again. At least tell me the truth. They say confession is good for the soul." Cypress sat up and leaned over me, blocking the sun.

Confession may be good for the soul, but it's lousy for the bank account. I saw no reason to concede. When you're told every day that it might be your last, well, I made my choice. Why should I feed this egomaniac's conceit?

Instead, I laughed. "You're right, Detective *Tree*.

All it took was a tilt of the head."

I stood and removed my wrap, adjusted my bikini, and winked at the good detective before I dashed into the waves.

The End

Looking for a new adventure, Renee recently moved to Myrtle Beach South Carolina. A storyteller from a very early age, an avid reader, and with an education and background in business and accounting, becoming a writer only made sense. And writing mysteries pure logic. That some of her stories mirror her life, only coincidence. Honest!
www.yolandarenee.blogspot.com
www.facebook.com/yolandarenee
www.twitter.com/yolandarenee

Reset
By Tara Tyler

Do you ever wish you could go back in time to change the past? I don't recommend it. When one goes back in time, a similar outcome inevitably takes its place. Balance and the natural order are always preserved. – Finn Zander, Time Traveler

Another family went missing yesterday. That makes five. It's been all over the internet. Indy is a pretty big city, but this family lived close to us. We knew the Jacobs. Sami, the daughter, went to my brother's high school. I wonder what's going on. Even the FBI is stumped.

The weird thing is: they all disappeared while having dinner together.

Since my family is never in the same location at the same time, I'd say we're safe. Who'd want my crazy family anyway? My sixteen-year-old brother Cole is obnoxious; my dad, Devin, is a total tech-head, always on one device or another for "work;" and my mom, Sarah, is too busy with her multi-tasking and never-ending projects to worry about what the rest of us are doing. I think I'm the only semi-normal one. But I hear the teenage years are when you start to lose your mind.

After seeing how the rest of my family acts, I'm going to do everything I can to keep that from happening when I turn thirteen next month.

Seeing my friend wave to me from across the food court, I roll my eyes and point at my mom. I usually enjoy going to the mall, but today, I was dragged along to help run errands. Mom is determined to get a million things done in one day. She probably wants to set a world record and check that off her to-do list, too.

"Mom, can I go to Abercrombie with Leena?"

"Casey, you know I need your help today. We only have thirty minutes, then I have to drop off the gift basket, pick up your brother, and you have a lesson. Ugh, I wish there were more hours in the day!"

"I could skip piano today."

She slams on the brakes from her brisk walking and spins around to glare at me. "Casey Rachael Carter. We pay good money for those lessons, which you begged for, by the way. You will finish what you started. At least through the end of the year."

"I know. Sorry."

Lingering, she purses her lips and scrunches her brow at me. I know she doesn't like to snap like that. It's just so easy to push her buttons. I shrug and smile at her. It helps a little. She sighs and takes off again.

I have to double-step to keep up with her. She really needs to take some time off from everything. Her head is going to explode one of these days. Most of this stuff can wait. But she can't stop. She's go-go-go.

She leads us to Crate & Barrel and pauses long enough to hand me a small, cloth-wrapped package. It's heavier than it looks.

"I have to pick out a wedding gift for your cousin. While I'm in there, I want you to drop this off next door at the Time Keeper. All you have to do is fill out a work order ticket to get this antique clock fixed. It should only take you a minute. Text me when you're done, and I'll let you know where I am in the store. Okay?"

"Sure." I nod and take the package. We should just give her this clock and knock out both errands at once.

"Please be careful. It's very old."

"I got it, Mom."

"I know you do. Listen, if we have time, we can grab some Cinnabites on the way out."

"Sounds good."

She smiles and shoos me toward the small, dark clock shop.

Shaking my head, I turn and go inside.

The door jingles. The place is empty, musty, and quiet. Except for the ticking. Tick, tock, tick, tock. It gets louder the deeper I walk into the store. As I reach the register, I hear a commotion from the back room: metallic tinkering, then a loud clang, followed by a curse.

I smirk. "Hello? Anyone in there?"

A hunched-over older man, with thick round glasses and a plastic green visor resting on his forehead, shuffles in from the back. He scratches his thinly covered, white-haired head and mumbles to himself as he searches through drawers and cabinets. I don't think he realizes I'm here.

"Excuse me. Sir?"

"Hold your horses, girl. Can't you see I'm busy?"

My eyes pop wider and I huff a laugh. He didn't even look at me. Not very polite. But now, I'm curious. I look around the store and wait, carefully holding mom's package.

What's so special about all these old clocks when everyone uses their phones to check the time? Clocks hang on the walls, sit on shelves, and four grandfather clocks stand guard over the little ones in the four corners of the shop. I'd get a headache if I had to stay in here too long, listening to them click, clack and tick, tock. Then I notice the time. It's 3:40. I sure don't want to be here when the hour strikes!

The man finally finds what he's looking for—some

kind of small, pointy tool. He sets it down and decides to give me the time of day after adjusting his glasses.

"Hmm. Very interesting. What brings you here this day, my dear?"

I set the clock on the counter. "I think it's broken."

He rubs his chin and squints up at me through the slit between his glasses and the green visor. The way his back bends makes him appear shorter, so I can look him straight in the eye.

He refocuses and delicately opens the package. After inspecting it for only a few seconds, he nods. "It's an Ansonia Royal Bonn. I'd say it was crafted around 1900. Don't see many of these come through my door." He lifts it up and gazes at it like it's a crystal ball that's going to tell him the future from the past.

"Can you fix it?"

He snaps out of his trance and sets the clock back down on the counter. "Of course I can fix it. That's what I do."

Frowning at me, like I'm a clock he can't fix, he points behind me.

"My dear, would you get that tool for me, please?"

I follow the direction of his boney finger to a metal doohickey over on another counter. I don't know why he needs me to get it. But he's old, so I humor him. It's just a metal rod. Strange tool with no handle or pointy end or anything. I shrug and pick it up.

The crazy thing buzzes, vibrating in my hand, and I drop it.

The old man's eyes light up. "Oh my heavens!"

I tilt my head at him. "Hey. Was that some kind of trick?"

"No. Sorry, my dear. It must have short in it. It's a battery tester."

Whatever. I've had enough of this old timer and his old clocks.

"My mom said I had to fill out a form or something?"

"Yes, yes." He opens a drawer and pushes the form toward me on the counter. "Everyone's in such a hurry. Need to slow down and enjoy the time you've got. Never know when it will run out. It flies by just like that." He snaps his fingers sharply.

All the clocks bing, bong, and gong their chimes. I cover my ears. Four o'clock already? The loud ding dongs don't last long. I check my phone. Only 3:45.

Before I can ask, he answers with a flat grin, "They chime every quarter hour."

"Oh." I finish filling out the form and scoot out of there before they go off again. He's probably crazy from listening to those things all day.

* * *

Miracle of miracles, our family is going to sit down to a late dinner together tonight. It kind of creeps me out, especially with all the dinner disappearances. Then again, what are the odds my family would be chosen? And it's later than the normal dinner hour. But still...

I consider asking my mom about it, then change my mind when Cole bounds downstairs. I'd never hear the end of it if he found out I was afraid of us all eating dinner together.

"Mom, can I go out after we eat? My friends and I need to study for a Chemistry test."

Sure he does.

But Mom falls for it. "After you take the garbage out. And I'd like you to be home by ten-thirty."

"No problem."

As he breezes past me through the kitchen and on to the family room, he messes up my hair and winks. He's so proud of himself for pulling another one over on Mom, and now he's going to butter up Dad by sitting with him and making lame comments about whatever's on TV. I wonder if they know he's probably not going to study. And if Cole knows they know, why

106

does he lie? They have a deranged relationship.

In the other room, I hear Cole and my dad laugh. Just as I thought. He has them both fooled. I wish they paid more attention to what's really going on. I bet he's meeting his girlfriend.

"Casey, can you set the table?"

I blink. "Yeah, sure." I also don't know why it bothers me so much.

* * *

During dinner, my mom makes us put our phones in a basket. Some new thing she's trying. At first, it's all awkward silence. My mom tries asking us questions, like how's school and our friends. We give short answers. Those are things parents don't understand and would probably lecture us about if we told them.

Then my dad gets us going by teasing Cole about his driving. We all add our personal near-death experiences with Cole behind the wheel. By the time we finish, Mom's experiment seems to be a success. I actually feel like our family is a little bit closer.

Just in time to ruin our good family vibe, someone knocks on the door.

I jump out of my skin and look wide-eyed at everyone. No one else seems concerned. Don't they watch the news?

Cole laughs and hops up, "Don't worry Casey, I got it. If it's the Boogeyman, I'll take care of him."

My mom starts to clear the table.

I look after her with worried eyes. What if it's someone here to kidnap us? Why are they all acting so normal? Hard to believe I'm complaining about that.

My dad puts his hand on mine and I freak for a second, jerking around to look at him. My heart is beating so fast.

"Hey. It's okay, Case. Probably a Girl Scout selling

cookies."

We hear mumbled voices, and the door closes. Cole returns to the dining room. Before I can breathe a sigh of relief, he steps to the side and reveals a short, older man behind him who's holding a small package. I squint at him. It's the clock store guy. What's he doing here?

Cole introduces him, "This is Mr. Zander. He has something for Mom and Casey."

My dad scrunches his eyebrows together. "Hello, sir. Can we help you?"

Mom re-enters and blinks at him. "Oh, is that my clock? You didn't have to deliver it."

But when he answers, he looks right at me, "Yes. Such a rare find." I get a chill and my lip curls. Creepy.

He sets the package on the table and unwraps it as he continues, "It needed my immediate attention. And it was so special, I wanted to present it personally."

Mom puts a hand to her chest. "Oh? How nice. It's been in the family for generations, but I had no idea it was rare."

"Is it worth a lot of money?" Cole asks with a grin.

"It's very valuable," he says and glances at me again. I frown. Something isn't right. Who delivers these days besides food joints and drones?

My dad inspects the clock, crinkling his chin. "I never even noticed it before."

Walking over to him, my mom swats his shoulder. "Of course you didn't." She reaches for the small, white clock with delicate flowers hand-painted under the face, accented by gold swirls. It's pretty, but I never thought it would valuable. My grandma loved collecting tacky knick knacks, especially from flea markets.

Before my mom can touch the clock, the man holds up a hand to her. "Allow me. The expressions on your faces are the very reason I wanted to deliver this masterpiece myself."

Cole nudges me and whispers, "Guess he went the extra mile."

I roll my eyes, but his bad joke makes me feel a little better.

Mr. Zander takes a key from his pocket and carefully winds the clock. We all lean in to see it work again. I'm curious what it sounds like when it chimes. Maybe it plays a song. With all the build-up, I'm actually excited.

As it starts to tick tock, we all nod and smile at each other.

A poof of smoke comes out of it. Guess he didn't fix it after all.

Then everything gets fuzzy and I faint.

* * *

Oh, my aching head. I blink and rub it. I'm surrounded by strange smells and sounds. Looking around, I try to figure out where I am. I'm lying on a cold, concrete floor. It's dark. And the closest match for the smell is wet gym socks. Ew. Then I see the hunched-over old man and remember what happened.

Whimpers grab my ears from behind me. I'm afraid of what I'll see when I turn around. I don't want to. But I have to. Slowly and quietly.

My family is all tied up. They're sitting in chairs, backs together, with duct tape over their mouths. My jaw drops. I want to scream, but they all shake their heads *no*. With wild eyes and head motions, they plead with me. They're all trying to tell me different things, and I can't understand any of them. All I know is I need to save them. But why would the old man leave me untied?

I turn back to him. He's busy tinkering at a workbench. Maybe I can escape and get help or untie my family before he realizes I'm awake. Scanning the room, I see one door at the top of a high staircase, but no windows. I feel like I'm in the dungeon of a castle. Or a torture chamber once I notice all the sharp tools and chains and shackles. What is this place?

I start to get up as quietly as I can.

"It's about time you woke up, my dear."

I sag and stay seated on the floor with my legs crisscrossed.

He turns around and puts his hands on his hips. "Now, don't look so glum. You came to me, remember?"

I sneer at him. I came to him? Yeah, to get our clock fixed, not to get my family kidnapped! I'll just bide my time. I might be able to tackle him when he's not looking. He's just a scrawny old guy. I could take him.

"What do you want with us?"

"Not so fast, my dear. First, I must tell you a story."

I look back over my shoulder at my family and tilt my head with a frown. This guy is certifiable. It's no wonder he hasn't been caught. No one would suspect the harmless old man in the clock shop. I sigh and turn to him.

"Then what?"

"Patience, my dear. You must have patience or you will fail, like the others."

That gets my attention. I'll be the most patient pre-teen in this century! Especially since I have to wait for a chance to knock him out.

He resettles himself on his cushioned stool and begins, as if it's story time at the library, and we're literally his captive audience.

"Many years ago, when I was a young boy in Germany, I had a lovely family just like yours. I had a little sister and an older brother. And we made clocks. Wall clocks, mantel clocks, figurine clocks, cuckoo clocks. We were famous for our handiwork and requests came in all the time for special orders. Kings and Queens requested clocks from us. It was

110

our pride and honor to create such sought-after masterpieces.

"Then one day, after finishing a special order—a very large order for a banker who was having a party and handing out gift clocks to his guests—my father was so proud of us, he decided to take us all out to dinner and celebrate.

"But when we returned a few hours later, we found our shop had been ransacked and the clocks stolen. Everything in the shop was destroyed. My father was furious and heartbroken at the same time. The banker, who had already paid for the clocks, said if we didn't deliver them in the morning, we'd be put into prison."

How awful. "Wouldn't the banker understand?"

"No, child. The banker was not an understanding man. My father knew he would accuse us of squandering the money. We were ruined.

"And that wasn't the worst of it. In the morning, we found my father hung himself in the shop."

I gasp. "What? Over some clocks?"

"Child, times were very different back then. My father's life was over. He knew the banker would not only throw him into prison, but he'd make sure no one would ever buy a clock from us again. My father couldn't bare the shame. He probably hoped my mother could remarry someone to provide for us."

"Still."

"Patience, my dear. The story isn't over. When the banker came to the shop to collect the clocks and discovered what happened, he felt bad for our family. Being a widower, he decided to marry my mother. She agreed so we would be taken care of."

"Well, that's good. Isn't it?"

"Not really. He was older and didn't want any more children, having grown sons of his own. He sent my brother and I to a military boarding school, and my sister to a family to work as a scullery maid. My brother was killed a few years later in the War, and my sister died of typhus. Later, I found out the banker mistreated my mother until she died, most likely from his beatings."

"Wow. That's really a sad story." I can see why he's messed up. But why did he kidnap us?

"All my life, I've been trying to find a way to go back in time and stop that thief from stealing our clocks. That one fateful event ruined our lives. I've solved every piece of my time weaving puzzle and located the proper thread of time to arrive back where I need to be to prevent that horrible circumstance from happening, except one."

"I suppose that's where I come in?"

He grins at me. "Yes, my dear. You have the perfect aura of energy."

I squint at him. "What? How can you tell that?" It's more likely I was the next young person to stupidly enter his shop. Then I remember the news stories. "Didn't you pick some other families? What happened to them?"

The old man frowns. "Don't worry about them. Once we reset my family, none of that will happen."

"Does that mean we'll be stuck in the past?"

"No, no, no. Your future shouldn't change at all. The reset should only affect my future. We may never even meet again. Who knows?"

"I would still like to know what happened to the other families."

"No." He turns away from me. "I'm not discussing it with you. You will just have to do what you're told, or your own family will suffer."

I look back at them. My stomach is all twisted, seeing them tied up that way, so desperate and helpless. I know they feel bad for me, for what I might have to do to save them. But I feel worse for them. I'll do whatever it takes.

"Fine. What do I have to do?"

He grins, giving me chills. I shudder.

"Come with me."

As I wave good-bye to my family, my eyes fill with tears. I don't want to let them see me cry, so I turn away and follow the creepy old man. I hope I get to see them again. I hope I can do what he wants, and pray he'll let us go.

* * *

After a short drive in his smelly old car, we arrive at the mall. I'm shaking nervous, mad, and scared. On the ride over, he warned me not to attack him because his basement was rigged to explode if he didn't return within a set amount of time.

We enter the back door to his clock shop. What could we possibly be doing here?

Does he want me to be a little elf and build or fix some clocks? I'm much better at breaking mechanical things than fixing them.

The back room of his shop is cramped, cluttered, and dusty. There are shelves and cupboards with drawers of all sizes along two walls and a counter with tools scattered on it. He holds up his hand for me to wait as he shuffles over to something huge under a tarp. it takes up half the space of the small room.

He tugs off the tarp, revealing a huge clock. The top is a glass dome with metal rings circling inside each other, and I can see some of the inner gears turning too. The base looks like a fancy elevator chamber with curvy metal decorated doors that slide open from the middle. Above them is the clock face. It's almost as wide as the base and glows like the moon.

It's amazing to watch it work. If I wasn't afraid for my family's life, I'd be impressed.

I wonder how long he's been working on it. I can't

imagine he does much business, so this must be where he spends most of his time.

But again, I wonder. Why am I here?

He whispers in my ear, spooking me, "It's magnificent, isn't it?" He must've sidled up next to me while I was staring at the huge mega-clock.

"I guess."

"Do you know what this is?"

"A really big clock?" It can't be what I think it is, so I assume it's a special order. Does he need me to climb inside and fix something? I'm tired of his dramatics. I wish he'd get to the point.

"It's a time machine, my dear."

Sure it is. "Does it work?"

"Of course it works, with the proper aura of energy to power it."

I guess that means me. "Is it safe? Have you tested it?"

He scuffles over to the machine and fiddles with some controls, making the doors open.

"Time to go." He spreads his arm for me to enter.

"Wait. What am I supposed to do when I get there?"

"Don't worry. I'm coming with you, my dear. Now, please. Get in."

I sigh and go inside. No fighting it. I really hope it works, for my family's sake.

Cushioned benches with metal arm rests between the seats line the small chamber, two on each side. At least we get to time travel in comfort.

As I sit down, he enters and pushes some controls near the doors. I pay attention, in case I need to make a quick getaway. Maybe I can leave him trapped back in time.

He sets the date, time, and place. Looks like we're going to the early twentieth century, 1939, in Bonn, Germany. If this fancy microwave doesn't zap us out of existence first.

The doors shut, and he takes a seat across from me. His grin is wide and scary. I want to get this over with so I can have my dysfunctional family back. I never knew how good I had it.

"Hold on, my dear."

I grasp the metal armrests and the time machine starts to rumble and vibrate.

After a minute, I shake my head. I can't take much more of this.

The old man sees me start to let go. "No, you must hold on!"

I squint at him, but firm my grip. My teeth chatter. My whole body is convulsing, like I'm on some crazy carnival ride that feels like it's going to break.

Finally it stops. It was only a few minutes, but it felt like two hours. My body is still pulsating as if the machine was still on.

"Can I let go now?"

He hops up and checks the control panel. "Yes, my dear. We have arrived."

The doors whoosh open. We're at the edge of a field. The sun shines brightly inside.

Though I'm sure I know the answer, I ask anyway, "Where are we?"

"My hometown. The day of the robbery."

"Are you sure?" It looks like a normal field.

"Come out and take a look."

I step out and see regular trees ahead of us. But around the corner on the other side of the time machine, there's a drop off, giving us a good view of a beautiful sprawling city, straddling a large river. There is a lot of activity on the streets and in the water. It looks like a nice place to live, for this time period. But I know what's going to happen in a few short years. Wouldn't it be nice if we could stop that from happening?

After the old man covers up the time machine, he

approaches me and puts out his hand.

"Casey, will you come and help me save my family?"

I didn't think he knew my name. I wish I could forget his. "As long as it helps me save mine."

With a sigh, I take his offered hand and follow him down the hillside into town.

* * *

We are definitely in Germany. No one speaks a word of English. And my clothes—jeans, a t-shirt, and tennis shoes—are getting some strange looks. I'm glad it's warm, since I don't have a coat or money. I hope this doesn't take too long.

After weaving through a few streets, we stop in front of a shop with a clock on the sign that says "Zanders." This must be the place. He starts to go in, but I tug on his hand.

"You shouldn't interact with your family. You might change too much. I don't think we could convince your parents to stay home, since we're strangers. We should wait until the robber comes and stop him." I don't think he had a plan past getting here.

He frowns down at me, and thinks for a moment. Glancing in the window, he sighs and his face droops. There's a pretty blonde lady and a tall thin, man talking to a customer. They laugh.

"I suppose you're right. Let's get something to eat. We'll come back when it's time for them to leave."

"Sounds good."

* * *

Once we finish eating, he shows me around a few cool historic—current-day for these people—sites: some extravagant churches and famous buildings, like Beethoven's house. It's been a nice trip until I remember why I'm here. I still can't believe this old man has my family tied up in his basement. I wonder if he's lying about them blowing up if he doesn't get back in time to turn it off.

We return to the shop early and watch the family get ready to leave. They're so happy. Especially the seven-year-old boy. Mr. Zander stares at him sadly, knowing what's in store for his poor unsuspecting family. I bet that's him.

When they leave and lock up the shop, we settle in to wait for the robber, hiding in some shadows between buildings.

Not long after the family leaves, two robbers approach the door. He didn't say there'd be two guys. How are we going to stop them?

Mr. Zander points at them and nods. I guess it's time to foil their evil plans.

The old man pulls a gun out of his coat pocket. Maybe he did plan ahead. I don't like guns, but this is a desperate situation. I don't want to be caught empty-handed and search around for some sort of weapon. All I can find is a heavy stone. At least I won't be completely defenseless.

We go around to the back of the shop. He takes a key out of his pocket and lets us in. Wow. I wonder if he's held onto it all these years.

Inside, the robbers are making quite a commotion, breaking the clocks. They've already started.

Mr. Zander rushes to the front of the shop and shouts at them in German, *"Halt oder ich werde schießen!"*

The two masked robbers stop and jerk their heads around to Mr. Zander. Then they look at each other. One nods for his partner to take care of us and goes back to destroying the clocks.

The partner runs at Mr. Zander. Not expecting an attack, the old man fires his gun. His hand is shaky, and the shot misses.

I duck behind the counter. I'm no match for these thugs.

Neither is Mr. Zander. This was a terrible idea.

When the robber reaches the older man, he swats the gun away and swipes at him. Mr. Zander avoids the blow, but doesn't back down or run. He reaches into his pocket and jabs the robber in the gut with one of his tools.

It must be electric because the robber starts to shake then falls to the ground.

While Mr. Zander picks up his gun, the first guy stops his pillaging and pulls out a gun of his own.

They're at a standoff.

I don't have time for this. I throw my rock and hit the robber in the shoulder. He fires before he goes down, shooting Mr. Zander in the chest.

"Oh, no!" So, now the shop is destroyed and Mr. Zander probably isn't going to make it back to the time machine. If I remember right, medicine isn't the greatest in this time period. Now what?

"Casey."

I go to Mr. Zander and check on him.

"Unmask them."

I go over and carefully take off their masks. They could come to at any moment.

Mr. Zander sucks in a breath, then coughs. "It's the banker's two sons. He set us up!"

I return to Mr. Zander.

"What do we do now?"

"Tie them up. Then everything will be all right. My family will soon return and find these ruffians and the banker will go to jail."

"Can you hang on until they get here to explain what happened? Then you have to come back to the time machine."

"No, my child. I will stay here until the new events transform our futures. You will have to run to the time machine and go back on your own. As soon as my family returns, time will reset and the time machine will disappear."

This is all too much. I start to cry. I've been dealing with it all, but now I have to do the rest on my own.

"What about the explosion? How do I use the time machine? What if I don't make it?"

Mr. Zander's breath is ragged, but he grins up at me. "Patience, Casey. You are a strong and intelligent girl or you wouldn't have been able to power the time machine. You know where it is and how to operate it. I saw you watching me. And you were right. There is no explosion. Your family will be fine. Go back to them."

I scrunch my face at him. How could he...? How will I...? I take a deep calming breath. I can do this. I have to do this.

He nods. "That's a girl. I do apologize for all the trouble I've caused. I can't thank you enough for your help. I know you will have a bright future. Thank you for changing mine. Now, you must go."

I shake my head. Maybe this has all been a dream and I'll wake up and... No. I have to finish this. Mr. Zander isn't going to last much longer. Though I'm still quivering from all the violence and stress, worrying about my family, I think of my family and I pull myself together. I give him a nod. It's time for me to grow up.

As I leave the shop, I pause in the shadows and watch his family approach. The young boy runs ahead. He opens the door and a shot is fired from the shop, striking the boy. He falls to the ground. My heart stops.

Logic forces me to snap out of it. Though I want to see what happens, if little Mr. Zander dies, I might lose my way back home. I sprint out of town and up the hill.

The giant clock time machine is still there under the tarp. I whip it off and dash inside, setting the controls to return at the same time we left.

Taking my seat, I grab the metal armrests, powering the machine, and off I go back through time. I hope.

* * *

Once the time machine stops shaking and vibrating, I let go. I'm exhausted. I can barely stand, but I push myself to keep going. I need to know I made it back and my family is okay.

When I exit the time machine, it starts to disintegrate, vanishing before my eyes. What does this mean about me and my family?

I rush out of the mall and see Mr. Zander's car. I drive it back to his house. I don't care that I shouldn't. I've done some driving in parking lots with my dad, and he said I'm a better driver at twelve than my brother is at sixteen.

Amazing myself, I find Mr. Zander's house and race to the basement. My family isn't there. Where could they be?

I hurry back outside, and the car is gone. In its place is a truck, and next to that is an SUV that wasn't there before.

I spin around. This isn't Mr. Zander's house anymore.

I'm so tired. And confused. But I have to get home and see if my family is there. I hoof it, putting one heavy foot in front of the other. I just hope my home is still where I remember. Something has to make sense soon.

When I finally reach my street, I sigh with relief. Everything looks the same. The mailboxes, the cars, the Harris's dog barking. And there's my house. My dad's car is in the driveway. Joy washes over me.

I walk inside and almost collapse.

"There you are Casey. I was beginning to worry." My mom gives me a hug. "Are you all right?"

My dad is on the couch, and my brother is in the kitchen doing homework with his girlfriend. The scene is oddly nice and normal. The same, but a little brighter, and definitely more relaxed.

"I'm fine, Mom. Just tired."

"Well, go sit on the couch and rest. I'll bring you a snack."

I smile at her, not wanting her to leave. She has no idea all I've been through in the last few hours.

As I walk over to the couch, I catch a glimpse of the mantel. There's a different old clock sitting in the center of it. Not the white, porcelain Bonn. It's wooden with intricate designs carved into it. I lift it up and look at the bottom.

Zanders.

I blink away tears and chuckle softly to myself.

My dad raises an eyebrow at me. "You okay, kiddo?"

I nod and snuggle in next to him. "Perfect."

I'm right where I belong, and I'm in no hurry to leave.

The End

Tara Tyler has had a hand in everything from waitressing to rocket engineering. After moving all over the US, she now writes and teaches math in Ohio with her three active boys and Coach Husband. Currently, she has two series, Pop Travel and Beast World, Broken Branch Falls. She's a commended blogger, contributed to several anthologies, and to fit in all these projects, she economizes her time, aka the Lazy Housewife. Make every day an adventure!
www.taratylertalks.blogspot.com
www.twitter.com/taratylertalks
www.facebook.com/TaraTylerAuthor

Three O'Clock Execution
By S. R. Betler

The clock outside chimed three times as Mr. Devlin clicked the recorder on and took his seat at the metal table.

"Today is the eighth of April, at three o'clock." His words were crisp and biting, as chilly and sterile as the visiting room. "Will you state your name for the record, please?"

"Maurice Oyler." The chains clinked against the table as he wrung his hands.

"Do I have your permission to record this?"

"Yes."

"Then, let's begin, shall we? As you know, I'm Matthew Devlin. I'm conducting some research on death row inmates. Thank you for agreeing to see me."

"Well, you were very persistent." It wasn't a compliment. In fact, Mr. Devlin had become downright insufferable, and if Mo had to die, which the state was determined to make happen, he wanted to at least be allowed to do so in peace.

"I think you'll find, Mr. Oyler, that I take my work very seriously."

"I'm afraid I won't be of much use to you, then. You see, I'm innocent."

"With all due respect, every sane person says that on their way out." Mr. Devlin paused to rearrange some folders in front of him. "Some of the less-than-sane ones, too."

"Right." Mo licked his lips and leaned forward, making sure their eyes met. "But I'm telling the truth. I didn't kill my wife."

Mr. Devlin hummed in the back of his throat, and

Mo slumped against his chair. It wasn't like anyone else had believed him, so what did he expect?

"Why don't we just start from the beginning?" Mr. Devlin opened a folder and skimmed the first page. "So, it was Wednesday, May 15th. Tell me about that morning."

Mo suppressed the urge to roll his eyes, but he couldn't stop the sigh that slipped out. He must have told the story to a million people by now. To repeat it again made him want to scream. Still, he had agreed to the interview. No one had forced him. Even if it wouldn't save him—nothing could save him at this point—at least he could tell his story one last time. *Someone* should know the truth.

"Fine. So, May 15th." Mo took a long, shuddering breath to steady himself. That Wednesday was not only the worst day of his life, but it was the beginning of the end. Thanks to everything that had happened, dying would be easy; it killed him a little more every time he relived it.

"I woke up with the alarm, like always," he said. "Jenny was still sleeping, so I didn't bother her. Did the usual morning stuff. You know, shower, shave, toast for breakfast, head to work. I mean, everything about it was normal. It was just a normal Wednesday!"

"Except it wasn't really."

Mo paused, intertwining his fingers and squeezing them together in his lap. "No, I guess it wasn't. But I didn't know that at the time. All I knew was my wife was sleeping peacefully and I was going to work. That's it."

"And what was your job, at that point?"

This time, Mo did roll his eyes. As thick as the folders were, surely Mr. Devlin had all this information already. These questions were just a waste of breath, and it wasn't like Mo had a ton of that to spare.

"I'm a stockbroker. *Was* a stockbroker."

"Presumably, everything was normal at work?"

"Yes, of course."

"It wasn't until you got home that you allegedly found the body?"

Mo gritted his teeth against the insinuation.

"I came home and found my *wife*, yes, and that she had been murdered."

"And who do you think would want to harm your wife?"

"No one. I mean, God knows she wasn't perfect, but Jenny was great. I can't imagine why anyone would want her dead."

"Except for you. Isn't that right, Mr. Oyler?"

"I'm sorry, what?"

Mr. Devlin paused to look up from the paper he was scanning. Without looking, he flipped it over and laid it blank side up on the other side of the open folder in front of him. He glanced down at the next paper and said, "There were witnesses that testified that you and Mrs. Oyler had a fight the previous day. If I recall correctly, you said, quote, 'I'd be better off if you were dead.' Is that right?"

A lump swelled up in Mo's throat as his emotions surged. If he regretted anything, it was what he'd said in the heat of the moment. Even now, those words eviscerated him and made it hard to breathe. Is that what Jenny felt as he said them? That's what he'd intended anyway, at the time, but now, he'd give anything to take them back.

"Yes," Mo whispered, shaking his head to dispel the emotions. "I said it, okay? But I didn't mean it. It was stupid. Probably the dumbest thing I've ever done. It was anger. Come on, everyone says things they don't mean when they get angry."

"I don't."

The tone was so sure, so matter of fact, that Mo had no doubt of its accuracy, even if he found it hard to believe.

"I say precisely what I mean," Mr. Devlin continued, "and follow through with whatever I say, because that's how communication works best. If I said I'd be better off if someone were dead, it wouldn't be far-fetched to think I would carry out a plan to make it so, don't you think?"

"Of course not! That's crazy."

"So then you were lying."

Mo balked at answering the question. No good would come of it.

"Do you lie often?" Mr. Devlin asked.

"I know what you're thinking, but I swear to you, I didn't kill my wife. And that's the truth."

"You have no idea what I'm thinking, Mr. Oyler."

The answer was so unexpected and cryptic that Mo had no answer for it. Answer it? Heck, he couldn't even decipher it.

"We still have some time," Mr. Devlin said in the same even, nonchalant tone as he flipped his folders closed and neatly stacked them in front of him. "You're looking a bit agitated. What do you say we pick this up tomorrow?"

The recorder clicked off.

* * *

Dong. Dong. Dong.

There was scuffling and rustling as Mr. Devlin set the recorder aside and put his folders in order. What sort of order, Mo wasn't sure, but it seemed to make sense to him, if no one else.

"I hope you're well, Mr. Oyler," Mr. Devlin said as he scooted around in his seat, making himself comfortable.

"Yeah. Just great." Mo scoffed and shook his head.

The sarcasm seemed to go right over Mr. Devlin's head as he sorted his papers, because with no sense of irony, he replied, "Good. Glad to hear it."

"You know," Mo started, pushing the words out slowly as he debated whether or not to even finish the thought. "My final appeal failed. I've only got a few days left."

Mr. Devlin raised his eyes, but not his head, from his papers to glance across the table. He regarded Mo without a word for just a moment before nodding. "Yes, well, then I suppose we'd better start, hadn't we?"

It wasn't the answer Mo had expected, but it suited him just fine.

"So you said everything was normal on May 15th," Mr. Devlin said.

"Yes."

"But you admit to arguing with your wife the day before?"

With less confidence, "Yes."

"And what was this argument about?"

Mo's head slumped into his palm as he sighed. Massaging his temples, he shook his head. "I don't even know. Something stupid. Just a silly lover's quarrel, you know? Like all married people."

"I'm afraid I've not had the pleasure, so maybe you'll humor me with more details?"

Mo glanced up between his fingers. No, the man in front of him sure didn't seem the marrying sort. Mr. Devlin was clean shaven, with his hair neatly oiled in place and attentive blue eyes. A solid-looking guy by all means, and certainly determined, but Mo couldn't imagine he got on well with the fairer sex.

"Look, all married couples fight. If they say they don't, they're lying. Little things. People blow up, say things they don't mean, and make up later. That's just how it works."

"I see." Mr. Devlin jotted something down in tiny, slanted, illegible writing. Without looking up, he asked, "But you didn't make up with Mrs. Oyler, did

126

you?"

"No. I never had the chance."

The writing halted, and the blue eyes peered across the table. After a moment's scrutiny, Mr. Devlin laid his pen down and sat up, returning his interest to the conversation.

"So, tell me about that afternoon. Last time, you said it was a normal morning, nothing out of the ordinary, but what happened after you arrived at work?"

"I, well, worked." Mo shrugged. "Same old crap at the office. It wasn't a bad job, but it wasn't terribly exciting, either."

"And during lunch?"

"I...ate food?"

"Is that all?"

Mo knew what Mr. Devlin was driving at. The files were right there in front of him. Mo couldn't read them, but he was sure they detailed all of this, all of his whereabouts, step by step. Nothing about his story had changed—the truth was just funny like that—and he was tired of telling it.

Pushing down his annoyance, he said, "I stopped home for a minute. I spilled some of my lunch on me and had to change before going back."

Mr. Devlin hummed again, a neutral sound that implied the answer was satisfactory but not surprising.

"And was Mrs. Oyler there at the time?"

"Yeah, but I didn't see her. She was in the bathroom and I was in a hurry. I just..." It occurred to Mo that this was the story of his life, more or less. Maybe minus the bathroom part. All his life, he'd been in a hurry, brushing things to the wayside if they didn't further his agenda. That wasn't what had happened to Jenny, he assured himself, but there were lingering doubts.

Mo was snapped back to the present by Mr. Devlin's voice.

"You just what, Mr. Oyler?"

"I just changed, shouted a quick goodbye, and was on my way."

"And this took place during the time frame the coroner listed as the estimated time of death?"

"Yes, but I—"

"Did you lock the door on the way out?"

"Look, I'm telling you, I didn't...What?" The question caught Mo off-guard. What bothered him the most about it was that he had no clue. "I...I must have."

"Must have?" Mr. Devlin raised his eyebrows.

"I did. I mean, I always do."

"You seem to be confused, Mr. Oyler. It's a really simple question. Did you or did you not lock the door behind you when you left?"

The chains clanked and jangled as Mo ran a shaking hand through his hair. He couldn't have forgotten something so basic, something he did every day without a second thought. Could he? But *someone* had murdered Jenny, and it wasn't him. The investigators reported no signs of forced entry. What if he had forgotten to lock it? What if Jenny's death was all his fault?

"Yes or no, Mr. Oyler. Did you lock the front door or not?"

"I...I don't..." The words wouldn't come, or maybe Mo didn't want them to come, because then it would feel too real and the guilt would come crashing down and crush him.

"You seem to be having some trouble remembering. That's fine." Mr. Devlin snapped his notebook shut and began collecting his things. "You take some time to think about it, and I'll see you tomorrow."

The recorder clicked off.

* * *

"We're starting a little early today. I hope you don't mind," Mr. Devlin said as he arranged his things.

It wasn't so much asking permission as stating a plan, but it didn't bother Mo. It wasn't like he had anything better to do.

"It's fine," he said.

"So where were we? Oh yes, you went home during lunch."

Panic rose in Mo's chest and settled there, making his breathing come in shallow, heavy bursts. It had taken staying up beyond the point of exhaustion last night—this morning?—to forget his suspicions, and Mo didn't want to go back to that place.

"You said you went home for lunch—"

Mr. Devlin was interrupted by the loud, clear echo of the clock tolling outside, singing out three o'clock, and he paused to listen. Mo seized the opportunity to move the subject forward.

"Yes, and then I went back to work and stayed until five, like always."

Mr. Devlin appeared miffed at the change in topic, with his clenched jaw and the intensity of his movements as he shuffled papers. Nevertheless, he continued along that line of thought. "When you got home, that's when you discovered the body, according to your testimony."

"Yes, that's when I found *my wife*. She wasn't just a body, Mr. Devlin."

The blue eyes glanced up, apparently surprised by the outburst. Mr. Devlin nodded. "Yes, of course. Will you tell me about it?"

Mo gripped the edge of the table to steady his shaking hands. It wasn't a moment he wanted to relive. In fact, he wasn't keen on rehashing any of this ordeal. Half of him suspected he'd wake up and it would all have been a nightmare, but that was just delusional and he knew it. Some nightmares were real.

"Like I said, it was a normal day. I followed the same routine as every other day. Got home about 5:30. Jenny usually had dinner on by then, but the house was quiet. I thought maybe she was still mad. Figured we'd get takeout. But then..." Mo's voice cracked as he recalled the experience. She was still in her pajamas, hair a dark, tangled mane around her face, and her skin pale and bluish. It was Jenny's face that would always haunt him the most, though. Her eyes were wide and terrified, her mouth frozen open in an eternal scream. Death had been horrific, and she hadn't faced it willingly.

"Where was it you found her?"

Mo cleared his throat and tried to push the image of Jenny out of his mind. "In the living room."

"And then what?"

"Then I called 911."

"What was the official cause of death?"

"Ligature strangulation."

"Did they determine the weapon of choice?"

Mo fell back against the seat and looked away. It was obvious where the questioning was leading, and he considered not answering. In the end, he turned back to Mr. Devlin and, with a sigh, said, "A tie."

"This was determined to be your tie, was it not?"

"Yeah, but I didn't—"

"Your co-workers reported seeing you wearing that very tie all morning."

"Well, that's good. That means they're not blind. But I told you, I came home during lunch to change. I slopped ketchup down the front of me, so I went and got a new tie."

"Threw the stained one in the laundry, I presume?"

"Well...yeah."

"So your position is that anyone could have

broken into your house, gone into your laundry room to get one of *your* ties, and then murdered your wife?"

"It could happen, I guess. I wouldn't know, because I wasn't there."

"How would they know to go looking for one of your ties in the first place?"

Mo held his hands up and shrugged, then let them fall palms down on the table in exasperation. "How the hell would I know? I wear ties. It's safe to assume they sometimes get dirty. Or maybe they just went looking for something and found the tie. I have no idea. All I know is it wasn't me."

Mr. Devlin paused to flip through some papers.

"It was silk, wasn't it?"

"Hm?"

"A silk tie?"

"Yeah, I guess."

"I suppose if I were to strangle someone, that's the sort of thing I would use. Not as sturdy as cotton, but there's something to be said about a good silk tie."

Mr. Devlin didn't look up as he talked, and Mo studied the bowed figure. He was polite enough, and the security seemed to know and trust him, or at the very least tolerated his presence. There was nothing decidedly suspect about him, yet Mo still was unnerved about the question. Something about the tone.

"Look, I've told you before—"

"You didn't do it. Yes, Mr. Oyler, I've been listening." Mr. Devlin wrenched his attention from the papers to glance across the table. "What's more, I believe you."

"You...you do?" Mo sat up straighter and scooted to the edge of his chair. Those were words he'd been hoping to hear for years now, but Mr. Devlin was the last person he expected them to come from.

"Yes, I do. That's why I'm here. Unfortunately for you, that changes nothing."

Mo deflated. Mr. Devlin was right, of course. While the words were nice, they did nothing to stay his execution. In three days, his life would be terminated, whether anyone believed his story or not.

Mr. Devlin had been watching him without speaking, but now, he cleared his throat and said, "I think that's all for today. We can do more tomorrow."

"Thank you." Mo wasn't sure why he said it. Maybe it was for the early reprieve. Or maybe it was because someone, regardless of who, had faith in his innocence.

The recorder clicked off.

* * *

The room was quiet, save for the hiss of the recorder.

Mo opened his mouth to speak, but Mr. Devlin held a finger up to stop him. Mo closed his mouth again and instead fiddled with his fingers. A moment later, the clock outside declared it three with a series of deep, reverberating chimes. On the last one, Mr. Devlin flopped open a folder.

"Why don't we talk about your court case today? You were found guilty of first-degree murder by a jury of your peers, correct?"

"Yes."

"Despite your plea of not guilty?"

"Yes. But the evidence was circumstantial at best."

Mr. Devlin hummed. "Let's examine it, shall we? You were known to be arguing with your wife. Some speculate you were gearing up for a divorce."

"Speculation isn't proof."

"Maybe not, but character witnesses are still witnesses. There was also testimony that you threatened your wife."

"I never threatened Jenny!"

"But you did make statements that could be

interpreted as threatening?"

Mo paused. Who hadn't said something threatening while in the throes of anger? There wasn't a person alive. Then again, most of those people weren't subsequently charged with murder, either.

"I guess so, if that's how they chose to interpret them," Mo begrudgingly admitted.

"Which gives you motive," Mr. Devlin continued without missing a beat. "And *that* brings us to opportunity. You admit to going home midday."

"Yes, to change, like I said."

"To change out of the tie that was conveniently used as the murder weapon and into a new one. Your coworkers testified to this fact."

"I told you, I spilled something on it."

"Yes, of course. You claimed that when you arrived home in the evening, you unlocked the door and found the house quiet, nothing amiss, and Mrs. Oyler lying dead in the living room?"

"Yes."

"The official police report says there were no signs of forced entry, no other significant prints could be found, and there were no signs of a struggle."

"Yes."

"Which led them to believe Mrs. Oyler must have known her attacker."

"It's possible." Mo had thought about it more often than he cared to admit. He'd certainly had the time. Nothing about it made any sense. No one stood out in his mind who knew Jenny and could possibly want her dead. Not a single person. The police report, he'd concluded, had to be wrong.

"And you can think of no one who would want to harm your wife?"

"No. Nobody."

"What possible motive could a stranger have for killing your wife?"

"None." Mo threw his hands up in frustration, as far as his shackles would allow. "I have absolutely no idea why anyone would do this."

"So what you're suggesting," Mr. Devlin closed the folder in front of him and leaned back against his chair, folding his arms across his chest, "is that some stranger decided to sneak into your house and murder your wife? There's no struggle, no forced entry, so maybe he enters through a door that was carelessly left unlocked. Maybe he's quiet, so Mrs. Oyler doesn't hear anyone enter, and maybe she's distracted, anyway, watching television. A would-be murderer needs a weapon, so let's say he picks up a tie, which just happens to be *your* tie, since it's your house, the very tie you wore that day. He, let's say, sneaks up behind her, throws the tie around her neck, and pulls it tight. Mrs. Oyler would struggle, but not enough to disturb anything around her, and the intruder doesn't touch anything to leave fingerprints. Well, except the tie, but of course, you can't get fingerprints from silk. Then, suppose he just slips out the unlocked door, locking it behind him, just as the clock chimes three, and goes on his merry way with no one the wiser. Is that what you're suggesting happened, Mr. Oyler?"

"I don't know! I don't know what happened! All I know is that I didn't—" The sentence lingered, forgotten, as something struck Mo about the question. "How did you know she died at three?"

"Pardon?"

"The coroner couldn't determine an exact time of death. So how would you know when it was unless—"

For the first time since they'd met, Mr. Devlin smirked. Mo really wished he hadn't.

"You son of a—"

Mo was out of his seat before the guards could react. The shackles around his arms and legs rattled as they reached their limits and his forward momentum cut short. Mr. Devlin never even flinched. Instead, he stacked and sorted his folders slowly, methodically, like they had simply decided to call it a day.

There was a loud scraping as the recorder was dragged across the table. Then, the furious jingle of chains, some angry shouts, and a loud detonation as the recorder burst against the opposite wall. The recording went quiet.

* * *

Mo shivered as the curtain lifted.

The chill wasn't from the bite of the cold faux-leather bed under him, nor the frigid air in the execution chamber. It was the blue eyes, glacial and unyielding. Mo could see them clear as day. Even though the glass was a one-way mirror, he was sure they were there watching him, waiting with glee to claim another victim.

The attendees whispered assurances that he wouldn't feel anything, but that wasn't true. Mo felt more now than he had in a long time. Anger didn't begin to define it. Rage. Fury. There were no words for what was coursing through his veins, and it was more lethal than whatever they had concocted for him. Despite his current innocence, if he'd had the chance, if those blue eyes were in front of him now, Mo had no doubt that he would earn his conviction.

Mr. Devlin was the one person who had believed his innocence. *Of course* he had believed it. God, how could he have been so stupid?

The first dose of liquid pushed into Mo's veins, but his blood was boiling so hot that he hardly felt it. What difference did it make?

In the distance, the town clock sung out a dirge for him.

Dong.

He was innocent.

Dong.

He knew who killed his wife.
Dong.
Mo closed his eyes for the last time.

The End

S. R. Betler was born and raised in New York and now lives in the middle of farm country, Kentucky. When she isn't torturing her characters or inventing new worlds, she's busy preventing her offspring and husband from destroying this one. She writes fantasy, mostly YA, and enjoys exploring life's moral and ethical dilemmas in her work.
www.twitter.com/srbetler

Center Lane
By Christine Clemetson

Hammond Stone swiped his forearm across the grimy mirror. He dabbed his index finger to the tip of his tongue and smoothed back a sprig of loose hair. Clutching the sink edge with both hands, he hung his head.

Focus.

8:02 am. Carla would just be getting into her Mercedes.

He straightened his shoulders and patted the ID number embroidered on his left breast pocket. Today he was finally going to a better hell. Whether she knew it or not, Carla was going to help him get there.

Hammond yanked a tattered notebook from under his mattress and thumbed through the dates and times on each page. On the last page, he circled 8:51 a.m. in red.

"I'll be there, my love," he whispered.

A siren pierced the concrete walls, releasing the cell gates. Hammond returned the notebook and donned an orange slicker. Prisoners gathered in the corridor.

Lanky Leo, the tallest guard in the place, brushed by Hammond. The smell of stale cigarettes followed. "Line up for garbage duty."

Hammond inhaled the moldy air and stepped in line. He glanced back into his cell for one last hoorah.

Nothing personal claimed his attention except one picture, the only picture he took with him. He knew exactly where it hung and how it felt in the dark. Taken on his college graduation day, it showed Hammond holding his diploma over his head with his mother beaming from her wheelchair. Who knew she'd die in an old people's home while her son served eighteen?

He squeezed his eyes shut. *Not now.* He'd kept it together for this long; he could wait another lousy forty-eight minutes.

Burt, his next door cell mate, nudged his shoulder. His breath slithered down Hammond's neck. "Sleep well, Ham and Eggs?"

Hammond fisted his hands. He wanted to punch the rest of Burt's front teeth right out of his mouth. Instead, he displayed a closed-lip smile.

"Fine, Burt."

Lanky began roll call.

Hammond studied the concrete wall. Rodents and bugs nested in the cracks, coming in and out from the cold as they pleased. They hadn't figured out yet that one day those frigid blocks would grab them when they weren't looking and suck the warm life right out.

A spider, with legs as delicate as black string, crawled toward a sliver in the ceiling. *Stupid shit.* Hammond eyeballed it and formed the shape of a pistol with his hand. With one quick stroke, he cocked the barrel with his thumb and pulled the trigger.

Bam.

"Stone?"

Hammond glanced up and grunted an acknowledgement.

"Easy there, Ham and Eggs." The words rolled off Burt's tongue. "It's only garbage."

"For you, maybe," Hammond mumbled.

Speak up, I can't heaaaaar you."

"Shut up, Burt," someone called from the back.

The gate leading to the last cell block squealed open. Lanky summoned the group forward. "Let's move."

"Ham, baby, how many of them cigarette butts you

gonna fork today?" Artie's bony arms hung through the bars. An old ass doing a long time.

Sweat puckered Hammond's t-shirt to his back. Forty-eight minutes and he'd be free. No more paying the debt for a crime he didn't commit.

His stomach clenched. Only one person deserved prison. Carla Meadow.

Carla ripped off every client that walked into Meadow Financial. As a business partner, Hammond knew nothing of it until the Feds burst into his office that January morning. The beautiful witch played the media and her industry friends to perfection.

And played him.

A black school bus marked "New Jersey Correctional Facility" waited outside. Hammond took his usual seat up front and checked the digital clock above the No Smoking sign. 8:25 a.m. Four minutes off schedule. Carla would be hitting the expressway already.

Dammit.

Hammond wiped his sleeve across his upper lip.

The bus bounced and lumbered onto Main Street. A woman and her brood of kids came out into the road, and a crossing guard stopped the bus.

He checked the clock again.

Too slow.

Up ahead, detour signs and lights flashed.

The bus veered onto another road. He shifted in his seat to double-check the cross street. They should have passed that farm with the broken down fence.

Oh my God. Were they going a different way?

Hammond drummed his fingers on his thigh. Seven minutes left.

Click, click, click. The blinker quickened to the beat inside his chest. The bus rumbled up the expressway ramp. Mile marker five passed. Then six.

Stop the bus.

139

The acid in his gut soured.

Finally, the bus careened to the side of the road and jolted to a stop.

The door swished open. Lanky and Joe got out. The third guard, Chewy, stayed in the rear. Minutes passed. What took so long? He felt Chewy's eyes piercing the seatbacks, as if daring any of them to stand or move.

Shouts echoed from outside.

He pounded a fist on his thigh.

Five minutes.

C'mon, c'mon.

Unlike most women, Carla arrived on time. Never even a minute late to a board meeting. Always lookin' hot too, smelling of fresh cut lilacs.

The bus steps shook under Lanky's weight. "Everyone out."

The sun smacked Hammond's face. Cool spring air rushed over his skin, the kind of air he'd never find in a cell.

Could he make it? The pulse thundered in his legs.

Lanky handed him a fluorescent plastic bag and a long-armed claw.

Draw no attention.

"You know the drill, stay to the side and no wandering," Lanky said.

Hammond fell in line, his knuckles whitening on the claw handle. He squinted, searching the oncoming traffic. Engines growled. A little green BMW passed, followed closely by Harris' cleaning van.

Soon, soon.

He edged closer to the asphalt. Wet grass squished under his sneakers.

Then the black pickup with the dented hood sped by. Carla would be next.

Gulping air, he tapped his fingers to his chest,

where his crucifix used to lay.

Our Father, who art in heaven...

"Stone—get closer in," Lanky ordered.

Hammond didn't move. Didn't breathe. In the distance, the white Mercedes convertible dazzled in the sun. Shiny black hair sailed in the wind.

The snap of Lanky's holster came from behind. "I said, move back!"

Hammond locked on the car. On *her*.

"I'm not telling you again."

Like a lion after sucking its prey dry, Hammond dropped his claw and strode into the center lane, lifting his arms spread eagle to face the convertible.

His vest flapped in the wind with satisfaction.

"Finish me," he whispered.

The squeal of tires buzzed in his ears.

Boom.

The blast catapulted him higher, higher, into the blue expanse. His mind drifted to that conference room. Back to the police cuffing him.

And Carla's promise to tell the truth.

At the top of the rollercoaster-like curve, his body jerked downward. As he sucked in the air, his stomach coiled.

And then blackness.

Something heavy pumped on his chest. They wanted in, but he wouldn't let them. Deep in his head, he smiled. No one was bringing him back to that hole. He was going where they couldn't take anything else from him.

Muffled voices poked through the haze, a shadow blocking the sun. The smell of lilacs wafted up his nose.

Carla? You here?

He rolled his eyes back, bolted the front door, and swiveled the blinds shut.

Too late for sorry.

* * *

Lieutenant John Medley downed the shot of whiskey and tapped his index finger on the dulled bar. The bartender arched the yellow liquid into his glass.

Medley pushed up the sleeve on his suit jacket. The numbers on his watch blurred. What time had he arrived?

Didn't matter anyway.

He slugged a gulp. The alcohol rode smooth down his throat.

Damn good police work gave him the perk to work later hours. What could possibly go on before noon anyway? The usual assault, maybe. Drugs? Friggin' Howard Lynn might show up at the park protesting. Nothing that called his attention.

Even Hammond Stone could wait. Another night in jail wouldn't kill him. The guy's guilt reeked from the very start.

Still did.

He stared at the flat screen at the center of the bar. A twenty-something with cotton candy colored hair pleaded with Judge Marie that her chihuahua hadn't bitten the neighbor on purpose.

Medley turned the glass in his palm. Of course the dog did it.

From behind, the door squealed open. The cone of bright sunlight flashed, and then the door slammed.

"Medley." Heavy footsteps followed.

The screechy voice pierced Medley's ears. The smell of spicy cologne wafted to the bar stool. "Go away, Wicker."

When the footsteps didn't retreat, Medley focused his attention on the television. Did Judge Marie really believe the neighbor invited the dog into her house?

"Turned off your phone?" Wicker asked.

Medley grunted. "Tell *Lieutenant* Benjamin I'll be

there by ten."

He didn't have to turn to see Wicker's slicked hair and pressed suit. Or his blatant disgust over finding Medley at the bar.

"Hammond Stone threw himself in front of a car this morning."

Medley's fingers froze on the glass. His eyelids struggled to open wider, burning at the corners. "When?"

"An hour ago."

"Can we get channel five on here?" Medley signaled to the big screen.

The bartender shrugged and clicked the channel. A pile up on the expressway flashed on the screen, followed by Hammond Stone's mug shot.

Wicker closed the gap between them. "You tell this guy they'll probably clear his sentence, and he does this the next morning? Benjamin wants answers."

Medley turned on his stool. "Doesn't matter."

"Yeah, like that badge you carry matters."

"Tell *Lieutenant* Benjamin to stick it up his ass."

A pause the size of an inflating balloon filled the space between them.

Wicker shook his head. "After Benjamin's direct order, you didn't tell Stone? Do you *want* to be fired?"

Medley returned to his drink and summoned the bartender. "Change the channel back to Judge Marie."

Heat burned in Medley's gut. Sweat pasted his shirt to his back. Stone's conviction had put his career on the map. Admit to the public that he got it wrong? Tell Stone he was innocent? No friggin' way.

He swirled the last of the alcohol in his mouth like mouthwash. "I worked this damn case. I built it on my own, got to the truth. Stone siphoned millions from over twenty-five companies."

Paper trail alone burned Hammond Stone. He'd made sure of that.

Wicker scoffed. "The co-worker signed the confession. Said Carla was the mastermind."

"Got plenty already blaming Hammond Stone. From investors. From the CEO of his brokerage firm. From other employees. Convinced a jury in less than an hour. No assistant to an assistant to an assistant, blah blah blah, can change that."

"So because of all that heavy lifting, this case will never, ever be questioned again?"

Medley pointed his gaze on Wicker. "This so-called confession is from an ex-employee who wants revenge."

"Carla Meadow was the mastermind behind it. Doctored the papers. Paid the others to vouch for her. It's all in this guy's confession."

Something shifted in Medley's gut. "She owned the friggin' company. What would her motive be?" Sobriety lingered at the edges of his head. But Medley wouldn't let it in. Not yet. "Don't believe it."

"I can't cover for you anymore."

Medley stared at the phone in Wicker's hand, as if the keys were waiting for him to make the call. "Did I ask you?"

"I'll give you one hour to tell Benjamin, or I tell them everything."

"That a threat?"

"You're a drunk."

The words dropped on the bar like the roll of a grenade.

Medley clutched the bar ledge and closed his eyes against the dizziness. Even if all hell broke loose, he'd still keep his job. His father used to be mayor for Christ's sake.

He'd convince Benjamin he had visited the jail to tell Stone the news. The guards would corroborate his story, as they always had. Then he'd fluff off the evidence.

Easy enough.

With Stone dead, no chance of the truth getting out anyway.

"Fine," Medley said. "I'll take care of it."

The rap of the gavel brought him back to Judge Marie. The crowd in the court room cheered. The chihuahua girl was going down.

Wicker opened the door and paused. Sunlight streamed inside onto the bar, watering Medley's eyes. "You better pray your ass off that Stone pulls through."

At the click of the door, he lifted his head. The warning pushed through Medley's alcohol-filled haze.

Stone's alive?

* * *

Medley popped a mint in his mouth and smoothed his wrinkly tie. Sweat toiled at his collar and itched. He clicked the button at the ICU ward, declared his identity, and the double-doors swished open. His worn loafers padded silently down the hospital corridor.

Wicker stood at the opposite end of the ICU wing on his phone. Medley averted his tell-all gaze. Screw Wicker and his threat. He needed to get to Stone first. Convince him that the evidence didn't matter and that's why he hadn't told him.

He flashed his badge at the uniformed skinny kid outside Room 503. Clark? Clemens? He never paid attention to the newbies at the precinct.

Skinny studied his credentials and followed him into the room. Medley nodded, pretending to support the young officer's due diligence.

The vinegary smell of antiseptic burned his nostrils. The *beep beep beep* of a monitor drew his attention to the bed. Stone's skin reflected gray against the crisp, white hospital sheets. A deep slash ran across his neck, with bandages circling his chest.

Medley's stare lingered on the chain securing

Stone's left wrist to the bed rail.

He mentally checked off the injuries in the initial report. Legs broken in nine different places. Fractured hip bone. Internal organ damage.

"Stone?"

No answer and no movement.

Man, he looked dead

Medley's shoulders relaxed. He glanced at Skinny, barely old enough to shave. "You the responder?"

"Yes, sir."

"How long has he been out?" Detective Medley coughed and opened his notebook.

"Almost two hours since they revived him, uh, sir."

"Did you take notes, witness names...?" Medley hated dealing with rookies.

"Some, sir, but it was a pretty cut and dry case. This man, uh, Hammond Stone, walked into the four lanes of traffic on the expressway. No surprises there, sir, except...that he lived." The young cop cocked an eyebrow.

Medley shook his head.

The rookie waited. "Sir?"

"Nothing is what it seems until a full investigation has taken place. Not even a routine parking ticket is cut and dry? Understood?"

"Yes, sir."

Medley stepped closer. "Was he conscious at all?"

"For a few seconds before the paramedics got there."

"Did he say anything? Why he did this?"

"He asked for you, sir."

"Me?" Medley folded his arms, feigning surprise.

"Kept saying your name, Medley, over and over."

"Not sure what that would be about."

"You're a legend, dude...uh I mean, sir. You nailed him with that case. But when he said..."

Medley raised his eyebrow. "What is it?"

"Said you lied."

His heart slammed the inside of this chest. "Lied? About what?"

"I couldn't hear, but he was acting crazy. His voice slurred...his eyes bulged and..." The rookie's voice trailed off, as if he realized the inappropriateness of his description. Medley narrowed his eyes. "Did you tell anyone else about...what he said?"

"I don't—I don't think so. It happened before any of the others got there."

"Think, dammit." So help him God, a rookie cop opening his fat mouth could cause months of damage control. "Other police? Medics?"

"No, I don't think so. And then he just passed out."

Good.

The door opened and Wicker's quick gait followed. Medley straightened his spine and kept his attention on the officer.

"Did you ID the driver?"

"Uh, just a sec..." The rookie cleared his throat and consulted his cell phone. "MaryAnne Clairview driving a 2015 Honda Civic, silver, sir."

Hammond coughed. A chunk of red mucus slid out of his mouth, oozing down the folds of the top sheet.

"Get the nurse," Medley directed the rookie.

Stone's eyelids slit open.

"You couldn't hold out a little longer?" Medley asked. He raised his voice enough for Wicker to hear.

"That you, Carla?"

"It's Detective Medley." Medley leaned in closer. "Do you know where you are?"

A smile crossed Hammond's lips. "You smell so good."

"You're at County General, Stone."

Stone twisted the sheet between his fingers. "I know the truth."

"That's right." Bile rose in his throat as Medley pushed the words out. "Detective Wicker here uncovered new evidence."

Hammond rolled his face away.

"This evidence could set you free, Stone. That's what you've wanted all these years."

"I saw the tape." Hammond Stone elongated every syllable.

Shit.

Medley forced a laugh. "You're not making sense."

Hammond bolted up, his upper body convulsing. Blood trickled from his nose. "I loved you."

"We need help in here." Medley slammed the nurse's call button.

"I knew you'd come back, Carla."

"He's hallucinating," Wicker said from behind. "Where's the nurse?"

Medley breathed the magic words through his nose. Nothing Stone said now would be believed.

"Relax, Stone. The nurse is on the way."

The chain on the bed rail pulled and clanked. Stone grasped Medley's hand, digging his fingers into the detective's palm. His eyes relaxed and the wrinkles smoothed on his cheeks, as if the clouds of an impending storm suddenly evaporated. "You tricked me."

Medley snatched his hand away.

"I loved you, Carla." Stone whispered, his words gurgling.

Rapid Response pushed through the door. Medical commands flurried across the bed.

A woman with a tag that read Dr. Marsi pulled a stethoscope from around her neck and shoved Medley to the side. "Please wait outside."

"No—no." Stone's throat bucked.

The slap of the doctor's gloves reverberated Medley's hope that this would soon be over. *Please. Let this end.*

Stone raised his torso slightly, grappling for the doctor's arm. His eyes searched the room. Tick. Tick. Tick. Then suddenly stopped at Wicker.

"Get...the tape...."

"He's delusional." Medley dismissed it with a shake of his hand. "He shouldn't be in this damn amount of pain."

"A video? Is that what you mean, Stone?" Wicker asked. "Where is it?"

The red in Stone's eyes blazed. "Behind...the brick."

Wicker stalked from the room, cell phone already at his ear. His orders to search Stone's prison cell echoed from the hall.

Son of a bitch.

Medley stumbled back, reaching for something to brace himself.

He's lying.

Medley clenched his jaw. A tape would kill his career. Not even his father's clout would make a difference.

He had no choice but to throw Carla under the bus. Tell them she had seduced him, lied to him, and planted bogus evidence to make Hammond Stone take the fall.

Maybe he'd even offer to go to treatment for drinking.

As if in response to Medley's plan, phlegm spewed from Stone's throat, and splattered onto the sheets. His knuckles whitened on the bed railing.

"Carla." Stone's voice hitched. "I need to make things right."

Stone yanked the doctor's lab coat. The metal on the ball point pen flickered coming out of the pocket.

"No—Stone." Medley paused before darting forward.

Stone thrust the tip into his own jugular. Blood spurted, his vein de-pressurizing with the force of a tire puncture. A gentle upturn formed at the corners of his lips.

An alarm blared.

"Code Blue."

More members of the emergency team barreled inside.

Minutes later, the doctor stood from the bed, snapping off her gloves. "Time of death, 11:15 p.m."

Sounds from the machines stopped abruptly. The staff whispers faded in the background as Medley paced to the window. In the parking lot below, blue and red car lights pinged off the hospital's emergency entrance. Reporters and cameras surrounded the area like waiting vultures.

He spotted Wicker working his way through the crowd. Medley held his breath as Wicker handed Lieutenant Benjamin a paper bag. The two men nodded.

He pressed his crusted lips together.

Jesus Christ.

A white Mercedes pulled right alongside the row of cop cars, as if it belonged there. Carla's endless legs sashayed from the car.

No—No. What was she doing?

She sauntered toward the two men. A shopping bag hung from her elbow, overflowing with papers. Even through the double-paned window at three flights up, he caught the determination of her gaze. Almost satisfied. She handed the Lieutenant the bag, her face shining, her other hand grazing ever so slightly across his shoulder.

Like old friends, or...

Medley's throat constricted.

Her smile locked the puzzle in place.

Carla had convinced Medley early on that she was innocent. Made him lock up Stone with bogus evidence and convince him that the co-worker lied about new evidence.

And then made him love her.

Hook, line, and sinker.

A breeze shivered the back of his neck, and he turned. A white sheet blanketed Hammond's body, smelling of detergent and new snow.

The End

Christine writes psychological thrillers and suspense. She earned her degree in Literature/Language and went on to pen stories that send you running for the covers. Her work has been published in several anthologies, most recently 30 Shades of Dead – A collection of mysteries from Sisters in Crime, and Tick Tock: A Stitch in Crime from IWSG. As a member of Sisters in Crime and Liberty State Fiction Writers, she loves to keep learning and sharing the craft of writing. When she's not writing, you can find Christine at the park with her family, grabbing lunch at her favorite diner, or pampering her basset hound Molly. And always with a coffee in her hand!
www.christineclemetson.com
www.facebook.com/christineclemetsonauthorpage
www.twitter.com/cdclemetson
www.instagram.com/cdclemetson

One More Minute
By Mary Aalgaard

After a restless night at the Women's Shelter, I was wide awake at 4:00 am. It wasn't the unusually warm and humid air for mid-October in Minnesota that kept me awake, nor the unfamiliar bed. It was the unending thought–how do you prepare yourself to break into your own house? Candi, my soon-to-be ex-sister-in-law, said that she'd text as soon as her brother, my not-so-charming husband, left on his annual hunting trip. Grayson had a cousin in South Dakota with 250 acres of land–swamp, tall grass, rolling plains–where they would go pheasant hunting every fall.

"He'll be gone for a long weekend," she'd texted, "Leaving Friday am. Asked me to watch Bo"

Got it. I was glad she was taking care of our Golden Retriever. He wasn't the hunting dog that he used be. Plus, Grayson's brother brought his new Springer Spaniel now, and Bo was getting older. He'd gotten more sensitive to the cold, and liked napping near the fireplace in the winter. Bo, not Grayson. Grayson was as cold-blooded as they get. He once described the rush of killing a bird in flight as a moment of supreme power.

No one besides Candi, my best friend Jackie, and my kids would understand why I wanted out of my marriage. Grayson Marks knew how to turn on the charm when necessary. He'd sweet-talked his way out of numerous speeding tickets, and at least one DUI. He could put on a good front with his three-piece suit, conservative but expensive necktie, and million-dollar smile. He knew where to insert a compliment, how to act humble, and when to sound authoritarian. A man doesn't rise to the top of the industry on good looks alone.

Dang. He could have been a male model. In fact, when we were in high school, the secretary sent in his junior photo to the local photographer, who selected him for a free photo shoot, so they could use his manly mug for their ads. Of course, I was attracted to him. Wasn't everyone? We started dating when I was a sophomore in high school and he was a senior.

My phone buzzed. "G sent a text: be there soon," wrote Candi.

That means I have precisely 12 minutes until he drops off Bo and heads West. I should wait for confirmation that he's dropped off the dog, but I'm feeling antsy. If he knew how close I was, he'd go bat-shit crazy. He probably knows about the Women's Shelter near the old depot in central Minnesota, but he's never been there. Did he suspect I'd go there?

Candi said that Gray bought my story that I went to visit Jackie in San Diego. She moved there three years ago, and I missed her terribly. She was my refuge and confidant through all those dramatic years. Grayson found every excuse in the book not to go see her, and made damn sure it never worked out for me to go on my own.

"Who will be there for the kids?" he'd say. "I have to work. I can't just take a day off because one of them has a headache!" He'd go on about this no matter what plan I came up with, and in the end, it wasn't worth raising his ire. He'd get mean and moody, first taking it out on me, then the boys, and I couldn't bear it.

I'd been protecting our twin sons since the day they were conceived. Now that they'd graduated from high school, I had my chance. No more guilt trips that I couldn't leave the boys. No more threats that I wouldn't get custody if I left him. No more fear that he'd go after them in retaliation of me. They were both six-foot-two, holding the line on the high school football team. And they were done taking shit from their dad.

I was too, but I needed an escape plan. Number one, bide my time. He'd freak if he saw it coming and tighten the screws, so to speak. I had to be stealthy, too. I brought a few things over to Candi's house, photo albums of the kids when they were small and special mementos of my mom. I finished cleaning out her apartment this summer. She would have been seventy-nine on Halloween. I loved her and missed her dearly, but part of the reason I stayed with Grayson was because she once said, "Divorce is worse than cancer."

No, mom, I thought. Cancer is worse. It took you away from me.

Number two was getting him out of the house, so I could pack up my most precious things that would be more obvious if they were missing, but only as much as I could fit in my car. Number three, get as far away as possible. He thought I was spending October in California with Jackie, so I had time.

He'd balked at my visit to California, per usual. "How are you going to pay for it?" he'd sneered.

"I have my royalty check from the short story anthology contest that I won," I replied in my sweetest voice. He snorted, but couldn't hurt me when it came to my writing. It was good, and he knew it. That's why he refused to pay for any workshops or writer's retreats that I wanted to attend. He was afraid of my success. I took a few classes at the library, preferring the ones offered during the day so he wouldn't know what I was doing. I could almost always count on him to be completely self-absorbed when it came to his career.

"What did you do today?" he'd ask.

"Oh, the usual," I'd reply, making a good show of folding clean towels in front of him, and dishing up a roast beef dinner with all the fixings. "I stopped at the library for the next Sue Grafton novel and found one you might like." Wasn't I sweet, always thinking of him?

"Would you like a glass of that Pinot Noir you like with your meal tonight?" I played the perfect wifey well, but my ulterior motive was to get him drunk and sleepy, so I could look over the notes I took at the workshop and do some edits on my next story.

He thought I was a night owl, but the truth was I took naps in the afternoon so I could stay awake after he passed out. Before we were married, I was a morning person, up before everyone in the house. In the first few years of marriage, I kept this up. I was in love with him, then. I liked to snuggle. I wanted babies.

When I was pregnant with the twins, things started to change. I was exhausted, so I napped. He'd call in the afternoon to check up on me and wake me up. I unplugged the phone, but he'd get pissed and yell at me later. Then, when I had a cell phone, he went ballistic if I didn't pick up right away. I had to give him some excuse for not answering, like I was in the shower, or had diarrhea, or something. The bad thing about cell phones was he expected me to be constantly on call. The good thing was I could be anywhere and answer the damn thing and pretend I was home washing his underwear.

I'd fall asleep on the couch while we watched TV, and he'd wake me up and make fun of me. "What are you going to do when those babies are born? You're not going to be able to take care of them. You're too tired and lazy."

When I was eight months pregnant, I was so

enormous and sore that I couldn't sleep much at all. Nights were a series of two-hour naps. I fell asleep on my left side, that would go numb, so I'd wake up and roll over to my right, hoisting my giant belly over and try to get comfortable. Towards the end of the pregnancy, I'd get up and sit in the recliner, reading, dozing, watching TV, and praying that I'd be a good mom despite my sleep deprivation and the stress I felt from my husband's constant criticism.

When Grayson saw me sleeping in the recliner after he got ready for work in the morning, he'd smack my foot to wake me and say, "I'm glad you got up. You and that enormous belly were taking up the whole bed." I was too tired to cry about it. He was a jerk, and I was trapped. Maybe he'll be glad when he has two sons, I thought. He wasn't.

Even though I had three days to pack up my things and get the Hell out of Dodge, I had a sense of urgency to get in and out of that house as quickly as possible. My stomach had been in knots for months anticipating this day. The place gave me the willies. Too many bad memories; the ugly words and verbal abuse still rang in the air and bounced off the walls. The house didn't even look nice to me anymore. Sure, it had gorgeous siding, a wrap-around porch, and professionally decorated interior. My mums in the front yard were still in bloom because of the warm Fall we were enjoying. But, it didn't even look or feel like home anymore. It was void of any warmth it might have once had. With the boys away at college, it felt like an empty tomb.

A flock of Canadian Geese squawked overhead, forming their V, an arrow pointing South. I opened my car window and breathed in the smell of decaying leaves. The trees were nearly bare, looking skeletal in the misty morning sunrise.

I pushed the garage door opener and held my

breath until I was sure Gray's truck was gone. I pulled in and immediately pushed the button to shut the door. Not that we were super friendly with our neighbors, but one might notice me and mention something to Grayson, which would tip him off to my escape plan. My plan was to drive South, first, then West. I'd let Jackie know when I was about a day away.

I grabbed the storage containers from the back of my Subaru and headed inside. The garage was attached to our mud room/laundry room. An unopened bag of Bo's newly prescribed dog food was propped against the dryer. The last time I'd brought old Bo to the vet, she told me he'd been gaining weight and that we needed to put him on reduced calorie dog food. He wasn't impressed. His arthritis slowed him down, and he took more naps. Gone were the days of him chasing squirrels in the yard and yanking me along when I had him on the leash for walks. He was my constant companion and my protector. I loved it when he curled up around my feet while I worked on my stories or read a book.

Grayson bought Bo and trained him to be a hunting dog. He did okay, but he wasn't as good as Gray wanted him to be. Is anyone? He quickly pushed dog care on me, then resented that Bo looked out for me and answered better to my commands. Once he determined that Bo wasn't much use as a hunting dog, Grayson didn't pay much attention to him.

Whenever our arguments got heated, Bo paced circles around me until Grayson blew all his hot air out or left with the slam of the door. My one regret was that I couldn't take Bo with me right now. Not all shelters or hotels take pets, and I felt the need to hit the road and get some physical distance from that man in order to think clearly. Candi would take good care of my boy until I got settled. Then, she could bring him to me, or I could come back, in the spring, after things settled down. Gray wouldn't hurt his own dog.

I paused at the new bag of dog food and quickly snapped a picture of it and sent it to Candi, in case she needed it for Bo. I headed up to the second-floor bedrooms to load up the essentials. I let go of any sentimental feelings I had for Mom's dishes, or Grandma's knick-knacks. If Gray breaks them in anger, so be it. I didn't care about the furniture or any larger things. I just wanted some of my clothes, the boys' memorabilia, and my cedar chest. My journals for the past 20 years were tucked in there amongst heirloom linens, along with my memory quilt, a gift from Mom before she passed.

My plan was to be really careful to not make a mess as I packed my things. I didn't take all my clothes, just my favorites, a few seasonal things, and spread the rest out in my closet to fill in the gaps. In the boys' rooms, I pulled a few things off the walls, and I didn't think Gray would notice.

My heart skipped a beat when I looked at the cedar chest. The top was completely bare. Had I taken the blankets off before I left and put them in the closet? I didn't remember doing that, but I was preoccupied with my escape plan, and maybe I did it to be prepared to get it out of the house. Did Grayson read my journals? I hope not. I was brutally honest in there about what was going on, a detailed account of our tumultuous marriage.

The bedroom seemed off somehow. Not that Gray was any sort of neat freak, but he did like to point out messy corners and dust bunnies. Nothing I did was ever good enough. It seemed like something different would set him off on any given day. He blew his stack if I didn't keep the bathrooms clean, so I scrubbed them good every Monday. He freaked when his favorite shirts weren't laundered and put away, or if, God forbid, I forgot to pick up his suit at the dry cleaner. I got smart and asked the dry cleaners to call me when they were done, and asked them to give another reminder call if I didn't get them by the next day. I constantly tried to keep ahead of his anger, anticipating anything that might set him off.

When I saw the unmade bed, his clothes strewn about, and dirty towels lying on the bathroom floor, I started to sweat a little. Part of me wanted to tidy up. The other part wanted to run out screaming. It's okay, I told myself. He's being a slob because no one is home to pick up after him.

Still, that bed. Maybe it was the bad memories again. Sure, sex was good at first. He was strong and aggressive, and I thought that was passionate. Once I got big with the pregnancy, though, he wouldn't touch me. He didn't like having sex with fat women, he said. After the twins were born, I thought I'd win back his affections by initiating the love making. Isn't that what guys always said they wanted, for the woman to make the first move? He seemed disgusted by my new-found sexuality, as he called it. "You must be getting near 40," he'd say. "That's when women finally get horny." My interest in sex actually seemed to turn him off. He'd brush me aside and go flip on his computer.

When that E. L. James novel came out, he chuckled at the title, bragging to his friends, "My wife can have 50 shades of Gray anytime she wants him, right honey?" It was a little gross. I didn't tell his buddies about his sudden drop in libido, or the fact that we hadn't had sex in months. Fifty shades of nothing, that's what I got, except for maybe those thumb prints on my arms. But they weren't love bites.

I wrestled the cedar chest to the top of the stairs then froze as I heard the garage door go up. My phone buzzed with a text from Jackie, "Hey, G. said you're coming to visit. What's the plan?"

Oh, shit! I should have given Jackie a heads-up. I didn't want her to get caught up in this if something went wrong. I wasn't even sure until this morning that I'd go through with it. Where did Gray think I was? Did Jackie inadvertently tip him off? Someone was pulling into the garage.

My heart thumped in my ears and my armpits soaked with sweat. Suddenly, that humid air was hard to breath. Would Gray physically harm me, or stick to his usual verbal and emotional punishment? Sometimes, I thought, if he smacked me around, broke my arm, or sent me to the emergency room, people would understand the Hell I was going through. What if blood poured out of my ears after a verbal slashing? What if those emotional scars showed up on my face as purplish welts? I wondered–how do you put your self-esteem in a sling and give it time to heal?

I jumped as I heard the handle click and the door into the laundry room open. I tasted blood on my tongue and realized I'd been biting my lip. I heard Bo bark and breathed again. It must be Candi coming over for his dog food. Bo sprinted around the corner and looked up at me. I smiled when I saw Candi behind him, but the smile froze when I saw the terror on her face.

"He's right behind me," Candi choked out. "He saw my text from you, and he's really pissed." The door banged behind her and my blood turned cold.

My husband stood at the bottom of the stairs in his brown Carhart bibs and blue flannel shirt, his blaze orange cap perched on top of his head, a growth of stubble on his chin, and his 12-guage shotgun resting on the crook of his left elbow. He looked like the picture in the ad for Gander Mountain hunting supplies and the next horror show villain all in one glance.

I swallowed. "Hi Gray. I stopped back home for a few things. I decided to drive to California instead of fly. I got to the airport yesterday, and with all the delays, stayed over in Minneapolis, then came back here this morning to regroup."

Grayson Marks didn't move, didn't smile, and didn't say a word.

Bo growled low.

"Come here, Bo," I called, suddenly wanting him further away from Grayson. Bo limped up the stairs, wincing from his arthritis pain. I knelt to pet him, desperately thinking of what to say to Grayson. Maybe the truth this time.

"Gray," I said, my voice cracking. I cleared my throat, speaking a little louder than normal. "It's over. I'm here to get a few things, and I'm moving out." I buried my shaking hands into Bo's fur. I felt braver than I had in years now that I dared speak my truth. I stood up, ready to face the verbal onslaught of my husband's wrath. They were only words, I told myself. Words that I didn't have to let penetrate my soul. I imagined myself inside a protective bubble. I looked at Grayson.

His eyes narrowed, and he still didn't utter a word, his silence more terrifying than the threats and abuse I'd heard so many times before.

"Gray," Candi said softly and moved a step towards him.

That seemed to set him in motion. He turned and shoved her aside with his left arm as he swung the shotgun out with his right hand. Bo barked. Grayson started up the stairs. My instincts for flight kicked in and I turned to run down the hall where I could lock myself in the bathroom and call 9-1-1.

As Grayson neared the top of the stairs, I yelled, "What are you doing?" Bo barked louder and started circling me like he always did during our fights. I tripped over him and fell.

Grayson cocked his shotgun as his foot hit the top step. Bo lunged at him just as the shot went off, taking the bullet in his own chest. He fell at Gray's feet.

I don't know if it was Bo's body or the recoil from the shotgun that made Grayson lose his balance. He fell backwards down the stairs, hitting his head on the corner of the newel post. He lay at the bottom of the stairs, out cold, and bleeding from the head. My ears rang from the gunshot, and I couldn't even hear my own screams as I held my dear, sweet Bo in my arms.

The world spun in a blur of tears, and I breathed in gasps. I looked down at Candi whose own eyes reflected my terror. We were both in shock, not quite believing what just happened. No one thinks their husband, or brother, is capable of murder. We both knew how volatile he was. We'd both experienced his anger and felt the grip of his manipulation. And, yes, there had been times when he said scary shit like, "At least I don't hit you," or "It's not like I beat you." And, yet, that's exactly what it was like. A verbal attack from Grayson left me trembling with fear, emotionally beaten up, and permanently scarred.

I held Bo close to me, his blood staining my hands and soaking through my pants. That bullet was meant for me. I closed Bo's eyes and whispered, "Thank you."

Candi pulled out her cell phone and looked up at me again. Grayson lay at the bottom of the stairs, blood pooling around his head. I stroked the back of my beloved pet, my protector, held up my finger to Candi and signaled, one more minute.

The End

Mary Aalgaard is a playwright, musician and arts advocate in the heart of Minnesota. She writes theater reviews and supports the arts through her blog Play off the Page. She teaches piano, writing and theatre classes. Her youth theater workshops in the Brainerd Lakes area partner with the community arts center and the community college. She writes articles for regional magazines, and works with both seniors and youth in multi-generational programs to enhance quality of life and build community.

www.playoffthepage.com
www.twitter.com/MaryAalgaard
www.facebook.com/PlayoffthePage

Heartless
By C. Lee McKenzie

October 6, 1871

Journal Entry

With a swath of pale pink paint across her cheekbones, her face glowed. Her eyes glistened in the light of my workroom. Even now, as I write this, I roll my head to ease the strain across my shoulders. Months of intense labor and still the final touches remain undone.

I can't believe I began a new project tonight as well. I didn't plan to, but I couldn't resist. She was unexpectedly accessible and a perfect match for my needs. So, in spite of being exhausted, I had to clean the knife before returning it to the tool chest, then wash every surface until all of the dark fluids drained into the hole at the center of the sloped floor. I hadn't needed the metal pot tonight, so at least I didn't have that to manage.

My last chore was to check the ice storage to be sure all was in order there. I'm smiling just recalling that moment.

Tonight, I spent hours longer than I planned, and I'd have been late to the dinner if I hadn't pulled myself away immediately. So very hard to do. When I'm not quite finished, I hate to leave.

With great reluctance, I drew a soft blanket around her shoulders. Before dousing the light and pulling the door behind me, I glanced back. I'm eager to dress her in the gown, and I must restore her hair straight away. It looks so alluring curled around the nape of her neck. I've named her Alexandra.

* * *

Police Headquarters
Detective Scofield paced in front of his desk. "Damn. Damn. Damn."

Sergeant Hawkins, clutching papers behind his back, only blinked, but perspiration beaded along his upper lip.

"When did this report come in?" Scofield demanded.

"Last night, sir."

The detective halted and faced the sergeant. "And nobody notified me."

"You were not," the sergeant cleared his throat, "on duty, sir."

"Blast it, Hawkins. I made it clear to fetch me immediately when a new missing person report came in. Young girl. Kenwood area. What didn't I make clear?"

When the sergeant didn't answer, Scofield waved off the next angry words ready to spring from his lips. "Never mind. Too late. What do you have so far?"

The sergeant handed the papers over and stepped back, silent.

Scofield read and hummed under his breath the way he always did when he was riled and thinking. "Exactly the same time. Almost the same place. From this description, the missing girl could be related to the others." This time his voice was low and dangerous and he flicked the paper with his finger. "Is she related?"

"Don't know yet, sir."

"Then go and find out!"

* * *

The Glenford-Leigh Estate
Mrs. Glenford-Leigh walked the length of the table. Flatware polished. Crystal gleaming.

"There is a spot on this napkin, Miller." She

pointed at the table and the butler at her side plucked the offending napkin and replaced it with one from his other hand. "Otherwise, satisfactory."

"Thank you, Madam."

He held the door for her, and she swept into the foyer where her first guests had arrived. The chill October air fingered its way inside the marble-tiled room, sending the chandelier into nervous chittering. It was one of the most impressive houses on the street. She cherished it almost as much as the memory of her departed husband whose fortune had made it possible. This time of year, Chicago days cooled quickly and the nights became frosty. Twenty guests were expected and on time. She held to the highest standards of punctuality.

It irritated her that Giselle hadn't come down yet. She greeted her last guest as she glanced at the staircase, a prickle of irritation flushing her cheeks. The girl was forever late. How she could be her daughter was a mystery.

When Mrs. Glenford entered the high-ceilinged parlor, the fire flickered in welcome and Miller had already served sherry to most of the guests. The small crystal glasses glinted in the gas lights. Conversations with punctuations of polite laughter assured the hostess she'd once again invited guests who would guarantee a successful dinner party.

She'd debated about Mr. Grayson. Rumors of his indiscretions made him the wildcard, but he was engaged in conversation with two of the gentlemen.

The Manfrieds approached. "Brilliant evening," Mr. Manfried said. His wife, who seldom spoke because she had the brain of a gnat, nodded. The woman was a bore, but her husband supported charities, so including them was necessary.

"I'm delighted—" Mrs. Glenford began, when the door behind them opened and Giselle stepped through.

Her sapphire-blue gown draped off her shoulders and accentuated her amazing gray eyes, her father's one contribution. She'd gathered her blonde curls back from her heart-shaped face. Angelic. Even the women glanced her way, some with admiration, others with nostalgic longing for their faded beauty.

Mrs. Glenford did not like Mr. Grayson's look in the least. He shifted his attention from his conversation, and while sipping from his glass, kept his eyes on Giselle.

The lecherous beast.

"So sorry, Mama," Giselle said in a hushed voice. "It was my hair. Madeline could not manage it properly tonight."

Her daughter's tardy arrival no longer the prime concern, Mrs. Glenford excused herself from the Manfrieds and took Giselle by the arm. "I have someone you must meet," she said, guiding her daughter across to the woman seated by the fire.

Widowed only three years ago, and by all reports wealthy, Mrs. Kent was a new arrival from Philadelphia. Mrs. Glenford hoped she would soon be a contributor to her favorite charity, the Orphan Asylum.

"Mrs. Kent. I'd like to introduce my daughter, Giselle."

The woman clasped the young girl's hand in hers. "Delighted. Such a lovely dress, my dear. You must tell me the name of your seamstress, and I will share mine with you."

Giselle took the chair next to Mrs. Kent and they fell into talk of fabrics and gowns. Mrs. Glenford walked directly across the room to head off Mr. Grayson, who was taking his first step in her direction. He'd not come near her daughter tonight or any other night.

October 7, 1871

Journal Entry

Last night's dinner party was worth the time I had to take away from my projects. I knew immediately that I must have Giselle Glenford. I couldn't look away from her the entire evening. The drape of her elegant blue gown accentuated the supple curves of her body. The flash of her keen eyes, a soft pewter, and the sound of her laughter enchanted me. Of course, it was her face that fortified my resolve.

I must complete my current project, and I've already decided not to proceed with the other. A waste, yes, but she doesn't hold the excitement that Giselle does.

I set to work early that morning, dressing Alexandra's hair, and then slipping her into the green silk gown. The pink roses at her neckline set off her skin tone perfectly.

Pulling her arms through the sleeves, I detected a slight imperfection in the wax along the waistline. It would create a bulge under the silk. On closer inspection I discovered there were more irregularities along her spine that needed smoothing; I'd have to do some remodeling. That's exactly what I'd feared. I should never rush one of my projects.

I'd no sooner heated the water than the church clock tolled two. Mrs. Glenford-Leigh served tea in exactly one hour. I had to set aside my work if I were to arrive in time to be included. I'm determined to make a good impression on that fussbudget of a woman and her daughter.

* * *

The Glenford-Leigh Estate

Miller entered the sitting room where the Glenford women were having tea with Mrs. Kent. "Madam." He held out the small silver tray with the calling card.

Mrs. Glenford took the card and immediately excused herself. Following Miller into the foyer, she greeted Mr. Grayson with a stiff nod. "What a pleasant surprise, Mr. Grayson. Did you forget something last night?"

"No. Not at all. I simply wanted to express my appreciation for your gracious hospitality." He took her extended hand and brought it near his lips.

The door to the sitting room opened and Giselle peered out. "Oh, Mr. Grayson." She smiled and came to stand at her mother's side. "I didn't know Mama had asked you to tea."

"I'm very sorry. I've come at a bad time," he said.

Before Mrs. Glenford could speak, Giselle stepped back and held open the sitting room door. "Not in the least. Please stay. Mrs. Kent is here as well. I'm certain you remember her from last night."

Mrs. Glenford clenched her hands, but looking toward the butler said, "Another setting, Miller."

The hour passed with talk of the coming holiday season, and Mrs. Glenford kept her eyes on the intruder. It was clear that Giselle favored him. What was a mother to do? A trip to the continent would be perfect to distract her daughter, but that was out of the question this time of year. She needed time to plan for the Thanksgiving and Christmas parties. Mrs. Kent, bless her, guided Mr. Grayson's attention away from Giselle each time there was a lull and her daughter's eyes rested on that detestable face. How unfortunate he was handsome and well-spoken, his manners impeccable. Mrs. Glenford was at a loss for how to manage this situation. It was times like these she regretted even more that her dear George had fallen under that carriage.

After Mr. Grayson left, she and Giselle saw Mrs. Kent to the door.

"So it is all arranged," Mrs. Kent said. "I shall send my carriage for Giselle about ten tomorrow. We are to have a day of it. We'll see my seamstress to give her some new ideas, and then we're off to the Palmer House. I hear it serves a splendid lunch."

"Mama, you must come as well," Giselle pleaded.

Mrs. Glenford had been so preoccupied by her concern with Mr. Grayson that she'd missed the plans for an outing. "Of course. I do want to visit our newest hotel." She smiled at Mrs. Kent. "Ten o'clock it is."

* * *

Police Headquarters

Hawkins waited until Detective Scofield read the latest report.

"This is all that you've found?" the detective asked, holding out the paper.

"About the girl, yes, sir. She's not related to the others, nor them to each other, but they are all of about the same age and physical description. Each of the young ladies appeared in the society columns within the last year." He shifted from one foot to another. "I got replies from two police departments that I telegraphed about similar cases."

"And?"

"Nothing solid, but last year Philadelphia had some society girls vanish. They never found them. Then something almost the same happened in New Orleans. Neither of them had much to tell me, other than they had never solved the cases."

The detective waved him away and sat at his desk. He needed to think, and he did that better alone. He took out the images of the four missing girls and set them on the desk. All of them were close to his own daughter's age, and that sent his pulse racing. The thought of anything happening to his precious child infuriated him. He slammed his hand onto the desktop.

"Damn."

Someone was kidnapping and, he rubbed his eyes now stinging with tears, probably murdering young society ladies. The similarity in each disappearance was not coincidence. What was he missing?

He rose and paced, then halted by the window to look out at the busy street. Carriages and bicycles. Vendors. A newsboy. Across the street a dressmaker's shop.

"Dresses," he said, fogging a spot on the window. He returned to his desk and picked up one of the images, then the other three. "Hawkins! Come in here."

October 8, 1871

The Glenford-Leigh Estate
Miller placed a small envelope next to Mrs. Glenford's breakfast plate.

She read the short note from her solicitor. *I must see you on a matter of great importance. May I call at about eleven today? Hector Bromley, Esq.*

"Oh, dear." She looked across at Giselle. "I won't be able to go with you after all. The solicitor has something he needs to see me about."

"I can cancel. We can go another day," Giselle said.

"No. You need an outing. I insist you enjoy time with Mrs. Kent and bring me back reports of that lovely hotel."

At ten, Mrs. Kent's carriage arrived for Giselle. Mrs. Glenford dressed to meet Mr. Bromley, then sat in the parlor reading. For a time, she lost herself in Louisa May Alcott's newest fiction, but looked out the window with irritation when Mr. Bromley hadn't arrived by ten past eleven.

"Tiresome," she murmured, taking up her book again and settling in. At the sound of the bell, she huffed and rose to meet her solicitor. When Miller opened the parlor door, it was Mr. Grayson and the hall clock chimed twelve.

"Mr. Grayson?"

"I'm sorry, Mrs. Glenford, but I was hoping you could give me a moment of your time."

She stepped aside and let him enter. Before closing the door, she said to Miller, "Send a boy to Mr. Bromley and ask why he hasn't come."

"Yes, Madam."

As she turned her attention on her guest, he spoke quickly. "I won't stay but briefly. I've come to ask your permission to court your daughter."

Mrs. Glenford sank into her chair. She wasn't able to reply.

"My reputation has been sullied by baseless rumors and nothing more. I would like an opportunity to show you and your daughter that my character is beyond reproach."

This was the last thing she'd expected, but she noted the sincerity in his voice and attitude, so she couldn't dismiss him out of hand. She rose once the initial shock had eased and she leveled her eyes on him. "I will give your request some thought, sir."

Grayson's expression troubled her. She couldn't decipher if it was gratitude or self-satisfaction. She would give his request some thought, but when her solicitor arrived, she would most definitely have the man investigated. Thoroughly.

* * *

Police Headquarters

What do you see in these pictures?" Detective Scofield turned the four images to face Sergeant Hawkins.

"Very pretty young ladies, sir. All very similar in face and stature."

"Their dresses. Look at them."

"Sorry, sir. I'm not much...but they do look alike with the roses and all."

172

"Exactly." The detective grabbed his hat and cloak. "Let's find us a seamstress."

They visited each of the families of the missing girls. And in each case the same seamstress had made their daughter's dresses. Once the two men had the address, they drove to the location.

A little after five, they entered a cramped shop. A woman straightened from her task and turned dim eyes their direction. With arthritic fingers, she removed pins from her mouth and stepped away from the dress dummy. It was draped in a ball gown, and they'd interrupted her as she pinned roses around the neckline.

The detective showed his credentials, and then produced the pictures of the missing girls. "Do you know these girls?"

She peered through spectacles set at the end of her nose, then looking up, said, "Yes. And their gowns. I made them. Each young lady had a special occasion, you see."

Hawkins gave his detective a slight nod of respect.

"How did these girls come to you to make their gowns?" Detective Scofield asked. "There are many seamstresses in this area of Chicago."

"A lady has taken an interest in my work. She brings clients to my shop."

"And her name?"

"Elizabeth Kent."

Hawkins wrote down the address and with the only lead they had in this case, they hurried across town.

* * *

The Kent House

It was a little after eleven when the carriage arrived at Mrs. Kent's house. The driver helped Giselle down from the carriage, and she went to the door. Mrs. Kent greeted her dressed in a flowery morning dress and not one meant for an outing and lunch at the Palmer House. Her hair, with its salting of gray, was pulled into an untidy knot.

"I'm so sorry, Giselle, I have fallen behind in some work." With nervous fingers, Mrs. Kent tucked a stray bit of hair into her bun. "Do you mind waiting until I finish?"

"Not at all." Giselle followed her into a pleasant sitting room with a small fire and comfortable chairs.

"I've made some tea and there are some biscuits. I won't be long."

Instead of taking the tea, which she didn't really want having just finished breakfast, Giselle wandered the room. It had few items of interest and nothing to read. The windows were shuttered, so taking in the view was not possible. The time passed slowly and after a while, she decided that she'd postpone this outing. In any case, it would be much more fun if Mama were along.

She was at the door when Mrs. Kent returned. For a moment she seemed surprised, as if she'd forgotten Giselle had already arrived. Then recovering her usual cheery expression, she said, "I...this has been an unusual day. Please forgive me."

"Are you all right?"

"Yes, of course." She glanced at the untouched tea and biscuits. "They weren't to your liking?"

"I've only just finished breakfast." Giselle reached for the latch. "I think we should reschedule when you're not so busy."

"No. That's not necessary. Really." Mrs, Kent guided her away from the door. "Perhaps you can help me, and then we can be on our way." She put her hand at Giselle's back and guided her toward a stairway that led to a basement. "I have my workroom downstairs."

The passage was dark and Giselle drew her cloak

closer around her shoulders.

"It is cool down here. Delightful in the summer." Mrs. Kent pushed open the heavy door.

The sharp, festering smell of the room brought Giselle to a halt, but Mrs. Kent was behind her and she couldn't back away. Giselle held her hand over her nose, hoping to staunch the bile that rose in her throat.

She was about to turn around, when a terrible pain radiated from the back of her head down through her neck, and she fell into darkness.

* * *

The Glenford-Leigh Estate

Mrs. Glenford took another sip of sherry, then paced in front of the mantle clock. "Unacceptable. Already after six." At the same moment, the doorbell chimed and she hurried into the foyer to greet her daughter. She would certainly scold both Giselle and Mrs. Kent for not returning at a reasonable time.

When Miller opened the door, a messenger stood there instead, holding a small envelope in his outstretched hand.

Across the front, her name was written in the precise characters she recognized as her solicitor's. She quickly unsealed it. *My dear, Mrs. Grayson, I am perplexed by your message. I have not requested any meeting with you. I hope all is well, Yours, Hector Bromley, Esq.*

He'd never sent that message. She steadied herself with one hand against the wall. All of her instincts alerted her that something was very wrong. Two women alone in the city after dark. She reached for her handkerchief and patted her forehead, then grasped the framed portrait of Giselle on a side table.

"Miller! Fetch a constable at once. Inform him that my daughter is missing." She thrust the picture at him. "Take this with you, and hurry."

175

Once Miller departed, Mrs. Glenford found no relief except by pacing. Her only child was her greatest treasure. She'd never be upset with her again no matter how tardy the girl was. Never. And she'd give serious consideration to Mr. Grayson's courtship. It was time for Giselle to have more protection than only a mother could give. *Oh, Mr. Glenford-Leigh, what I wouldn't give to have you at my side this very moment.*

* * *

The Kent House

Scofield sat next to Hawkins inside the police carriage as it dipped and rocked through the streets. The detective's mind churned with possibilities. Was it possible they'd find the link to the missing girls at this society house? Or, was this connection between the girls, the dressmaker, and Mrs. Kent a distraction that was leading him away from solving this mystery? If so, would it make him too late to save even the last abducted girl?

At Mrs. Kent's house the detective rapped the heavy iron knocker against the door, then listened. Nothing stirred inside.

Hawkins made his way around the front, peering in the first floor windows. He returned to the porch. "All shuttered, sir."

"We'll come back later, then." Detective Scofield came down the steps and the men returned to their carriage. "I want one of our constables to watch the house. Put someone on duty here as soon as we return to the precinct."

"Yes, sir."

It was almost seven by the time they arrived back at headquarters, and the desk sergeant stopped the detective on his way in. "A Mr. Miller's in your office, sir. He says it's urgent."

The detective pushed opened his office door, and Miller hurriedly relayed Mrs. Glenford-Leigh's concern.

Miller fingered his hat brim as he said, "The ladies were to lunch at the Palmer House after visiting a seamstress. Madam is distressed that something has happened to them."

Ordinarily, Detective Scofield would have turned this matter over to Hawkins to take the report, but the name Mrs. Kent and the word seamstress stopped him.

"Did you bring a picture of the missing girl?" he asked.

Miller held out the framed image of Giselle.

Young society girl. Gown. Slightly different design, but there were too many similarities to ignore.

He wrenched open his door. "Hawkins!" The detective said, his raised voice silencing the office noise. "Come with me." He was already outside by the time Hawkins caught up with him."

* * *

The Kent House

This was not as she'd planned it. She still hadn't finished Alexandra completely, and now Giselle was waiting.

She hurried to fasten Giselle's wrists and ankles to the table, careful not to cause her more pain. She never liked the girls to suffer. The tea and biscuits always put them to sleep, so when she began her work, they felt nothing. She checked for damage to Giselle's head, but she'd aimed where to bring the pipe down. There was only the slightest bit of blood.

Again, she'd have to work faster than she liked.

"I'm going to finish the remodeling for you, Alexandra, then I'll put on your gown and see you are comfortable in the green bedroom," Mrs. Kent whispered. If only her girls could listen and respond. She missed their voices. Longed to hear their laughter.

Kneeling before the figure, she gently ran the

heated rod along Alexandra's side until the wax smoothed over the ribcage. She examined the repairs she'd made to the girl's back, and nodded. "Well, done."

When the church bell tolled, she halted, surprised that it was already eight. By now Mrs. Glenford-Leigh had alerted the authorities.

She must be ready to meet the police at the door with shock and dismay when they told her Giselle was missing.

She had her story memorized.

The last I saw of Miss Glenford was at the Palmer Hotel when Mr. Grayson insisted he take her home at her mother's request. Of course, I was horrified, but he had been a guest at the dinner party, and Miss Glenford seemed so very pleased to accompany him. Also, he had engaged an open carriage, so he was most proper. What could I do?

All of that sounded very convincing.

On the table, Giselle moaned and tried to lift her hand. "Mrs. Kent," she cried. "Help me."

Mrs. Kent sprinkled chloroform on a cloth and held it to Giselle's nose. "Sleep, dear. I'll be back very quickly."

Alexandra weighed slightly less than she had before evisceration, but still, carrying her upstairs required energy and took time. If she'd been sculpted from clay and then waxed as in Madame Tussaud's, carrying her or any of the others would have been impossible.

Perspiration moistened Mrs. Kent's forehead as she settled Alexandra onto the settee.

She stepped back, her hands clasped at her bosom. "Lovely."

On her way back, she looked into the rose room where Daphne waited. At the next door, she gazed fondly at Catherine. "Lavender suits you so. I knew you'd be perfect here."

She hurried down to her workroom. And now Giselle.

* * *

Police Headquarters

A lame horse delayed the detective and Hawkins. By the time they'd hitched another to the carriage, Detective Scofield's temper had flared twice. Finally, they raced away from headquarters, careened onto the main street, and urging the horse to a fast trot, made straight to the Kent house. Gaslights flickered along their route. Feral cats scurried down alleys.

They'd come to a cross street when Hawkins reigned the horse to a halt.

"What in—" The detective turned on the sergeant. This was not the time to stop.

Hawkins said nothing, but pointed at the horizon. Ahead, an eerie glow brightened the night sky and black smoke billowed upward. The air was suddenly filled with ash and the heat of unbridled fire. From behind them came the loud clatter of hooves and the clang of bells. Hawkins drove the carriage to the side as two steam engines, belching smoke and scattering hot embers, roared past.

"Good, God!" Detective Scofield shouted. "Chicago's burning."

"It's coming our direction, sir." Hawkins swiped his hand across his forehead.

"Get to the Kent house. Now!"

Hawkins flicked the reins over the horse's neck and they raced toward the flames.

* * *

The Kent House

Giselle was still unconscious when Mrs. Kent returned and carefully laid out her knife. Peeling back the bodice of Giselle's dress and slicing open her corset, she laid thick towels along her sides and set a bucket at the head of the table to hold the organs.

Removing a clean apron from the chest, she covered her own dress and smoothed back her hair, shivering with anticipation. Soon she'd hold a heart in its pulsing last seconds. Symbolic, yes. But soothing to her own heart that still ached two years after his betrayal. She closed her eyes, remembering her husband's parting words. *I can't love you when another has stolen my heart.*

The image of the young girl waiting for him in his carriage remained seared in her mind. Mrs. Kent pressed her hand to her chest. The miserable memory of that day. Her heart battering to escape the confines of her bosom. So much pain. So much humiliation. His handsome face turning away from her entreaties.

"Beast," she murmured.

She grasped the knife. Opening of the skin was not her favorite part of the preparation, but it was necessary. All she needed was the exterior to submerge in the wax. A beautiful sculpture.

Placing the knife just below the sternum she made a small cut. She wanted to be sure Giselle was still in a deep sleep. The girl moaned, but then became quiet.

Mrs. Kent took a steadying breath and positioned the knife at the cut.

The loud pounding at her front door stopped her hand.

"Not now," she hissed and slammed the knife onto the table.

The pounding persisted, so she tore off her apron. She stepped into the dark corridor, then locking the door, hurried to give her story to the police. As she reached the first floor, the strong scent of smoke caught in her throat.

When she opened the door, two men pushed their way inside.

The taller of the two spoke urgently. "Mrs. Elizabeth Kent?"

"Yes." Her voice matched his in intensity.

"I'm Detective Scofield. There's a fire. You must leave here at once." He squinted, peering into the dim and smoky room. "Is Miss Glenford with you?"

"No." Then alarmed, she said, "Fire? Where?"

The shorter man coughed and covered his nose with a handkerchief. "Just about everywhere from the looks of it."

"Is anyone else in the house?" Detective Scofield scanned the room, noting the tea and untouched biscuits.

She looked up at the second floor. "Oh no!" She ran up the steps. They'd be destroyed. All her work. Her girls gone in flames. That couldn't happen.

"Mrs. Kent!" Detective Scofield vaulted after her. "Stop! We must leave at once."

Without a backward glance she shoved open the door to the green bedroom. *Alexandra. She'd save her. But what of the others?* She held her arm across her face, choking on each breath.

"Oh my God." The deep voice of Detective Scofield came from behind her.

Mrs. Kent held the wax figure in her arms. "I must save her. Please help me."

Detective Scofield bolted from the room and shouted down to where his sergeant paced, coughing. "Hawkins! Search this place. Now." He turned on Mrs. Kent who stood gripping the figure. "Where is Giselle Glenford?"

Her lips quivered, but she didn't answer.

"Tell me at once or I'll throw that," he pointed to the wax figure, "into the fire this moment."

Mrs. Kent bit back tears. "The workroom. Basement," she said in barely a whisper.

The detective ran from the room and bounded

down the stairs. Acrid smoke rose to the ceiling and an orange glow filtered through the shuttered windows. Then the roar of consuming flames became unmistakable. The fire storm was on them.

He gasped for air, but holding his cloak to his face, he found the stairs down. He pushed on the door. It didn't open. He turned at the sound of footsteps. "Hawkins. Thank God. Give me a shoulder here."

Together they hurled themselves at the door. It didn't give way. Again they rammed it. This time the jamb cracked a bit. On the third try, it splintered, and they stumbled into the basement room, the dark stench billowing from inside.

Detective Scofield regained his balance and hurried to place his fingers on Giselle's throat.

"Is she alive?" Hawkins gasped.

"Yes. Help me free her."

Fumbling with the knots, they untied Giselle's wrists and ankles, releasing her from the table. Detective Scott wrapped her in his cloak and lifted her from the table.

"Sir, you must see this." Hawkins had opened the door of the large ice storage cabinet.

On the floor lay the body of a young girl. Above her on a shelf were four human hearts, frozen.

Detective Scofield blanched, then coughing to clear the smoke from his lungs, said, "There's nothing we can do for her. Come."

By the time they reached the first floor, the house was in flames. Hawkins yanked open the front door at the same moment the ceiling collapsed onto the floor behind them. In the rubble lay Mrs. Kent. In her arms she held a melting body of a young girl dressed in a green silk gown.

The End

C. LEE MCKENZIE

C. Lee McKenzie has a background in Linguistics and Inter-Cultural Communication, but these days her greatest passion is writing for young readers. When she's not writing she's hiking or traveling or practicing yoga or asking a lot questions about things she still doesn't understand.
www.writegame.blogspot.com
www.facebook.com/cleemckenzie
www.twitter.com/cleemckenzie

Until Release
By Jemi Fraser

120 minutes until release

It proved impossible to paint nail polish neatly while imagining her fingers wrapped around that throat. Squeezing until the pulse ceased to beat and the life was gone.

Like her Matt's life.

Gone.

Four years, three months, and thirteen days gone. Less than five years to pay for the death of her son. Snuffed out at nineteen. Run down like he meant nothing.

It wasn't enough.

Walker had to pay like her Matt had paid.

Ashley took a deep breath followed by three more. Then picked up the polish with a steady hand.

120 minutes until release

Government was going to hell. Politicians these days didn't have guts. Not like in the old days.

Those idiots were swayed by the namby-pambies of the world. The criminal had a hard life. Boo-fricking-hoo. They deserved it. Paying a debt to society should mean something. Make the consequences tough enough and people stopped being stupid.

Early release for good behaviour was a dumbass idea. If they possessed good behaviour, they wouldn't be in prison in the first place. Easy to fake being good when there weren't any real choices to be made.

It was time to open some eyes. Time to remind

people that criminals belonged in jail where they couldn't hurt anyone else. And they needed to stay in jail for their full sentences. This early release crap had to stop.

George and his buddies were just the guys to take care of it.

120 minutes until release

Sean Walker glared at the clock. Two more hours before he could get back to his real life. He'd lost so much time. For more than four years he'd frittered away his life in this filthy dump. Wearing clothes that scratched, using humiliating public toilets, breathing the same air as men who were nothing but a waste of skin.

They owed him big and they were going to pay. Anyone who'd caused this. Everyone. The lawyers should have done better, so he'd start with them.

But first, he wanted a bottle of Jack, a box of cigars, and a woman. Or two.

Then it would be all about revenge.

110 minutes until release

It shouldn't still feel like yesterday. Grief wasn't supposed to be debilitating after four years.

Well-meaning friends kept telling Nita that heartache healed as time marched on. Bull. Shattered pieces of the past and future collided inside her on a daily basis.

First love. Forever love.

Gone.

Like yesterday.

She only had to blink to watch his body fly across the road and crash into a light pole. Broken. Smashed. Destroyed.

They said he died instantly.

They said he didn't feel a thing.

They said it was a comfort.

They were wrong.

He shouldn't be dead. The two of them should be looking ahead to their future. Buying their first home. Settling in to their careers. Planning a family.

None of it would ever happen.

All because of a man who was scheduled to walk the streets freely in only a few hours.

Early release because they'd decided he hadn't meant to kill. Hadn't meant to drink a dozen shots of whiskey or speed down the street at almost double the limit. Hadn't meant to smash into the man crossing the street on a green light.

But he had.

It was unforgivable.

And it still felt like yesterday.

100 minutes until release

The trick was getting the details right, in ensuring none of the rifle pieces were easy to identify. The human eye was ridiculously easy to trick, just like the human brain.

A soft smile, a tip of the head, a nod of recognition. That's all it took for Cam to bypass security and fool victims. Not much of a challenge anymore. It was becoming dull. Almost time to move on, find something new.

Not yet, because today held the promise of fun. The crowds, the protestors. Police officers and opposing families. There was always drama in that. And drama created confusion which equaled an easy exit.

The scene would have been cleared that morning and cops would soon surround the perimeter. Normally his jobs required being in place for hours before the event. Not today. Today, the timeline would be tight and therein lay the challenge.

Security would need to be confused.

The tools needed to be hidden in plain sight.

The pistol grip was perhaps the most difficult today. With a little creativity, it would pass as a water gun wrapped up for a nephew's birthday.

Wrapped in Sponge Bob paper and a bright blue ribbon.

The trick was getting the details right.

90 minutes until release

It had taken far too many months for Jake to realize who he'd worked for. *What* he'd worked for. He wasn't sure they qualified for human status. Not anymore.

For long years, he'd absorbed every scrap of knowledge he could find. Clawed his way out of the neighborhood where being smart got you beaten up on principle. He'd worked his butt off to get scholarships and worked multiple jobs in order to pay for food and a roof over his head.

Undergrad degree. Law school. Passed the bar. Landed an internship. Then a job.

He'd achieved every damn thing on his own.

And then he'd taken on the case of a drunk driver, although Jake doubted that was the only thing impairing Sean Walker's judgment that night.

Walker had been guilty, but Jake's job had been to protect him. Cocky, arrogant, entitled. Rich little snot who knew his daddy would take care of things.

Especially since Daddy had ties to all kinds of terrifying and illegal activities. Drugs for sure, but possible connections to human trafficking of the worst kind. Kids. A man with no conscience who'd raised a son in his image. A son with no moral high ground.

Witness accounts made Jake think Walker'd run over the victim on purpose. To see how it felt. To watch the poor kid bounce.

A more disgusting piece of humanity he'd yet to meet.

The case against Walker had been airtight. Alcohol level over double the legal limit. No mechanical issues with the vehicle. Eyewitness testimony. Traffic cameras.

Jake had done his best because that was his job. He hadn't walked away despite the temptation of letting the scum rot without representation, but he hadn't wasted a single regret when Walker had been found guilty of manslaughter.

He shouldn't be walking after less than a third of his sentence. Shouldn't be walking ever.

Maybe Jake would feel clean again when he'd done something to make it right.

90 minutes until release

After Sally's parents had been killed by a drunk driver when she was a kid, she'd skipped from foster home to foster home. Nice enough people, but not family.

Her parents' killer only spent months in prison before being set free. He'd left the country before she'd entered high school.

Tracking killers had become her obsession. She knew it wasn't healthy, but she couldn't stop. Someone had to make people listen. Someone had to spearhead change.

Through high school and college, she'd never touched a drop of alcohol. She'd spent the weekends studying and she'd earned three degrees. Her body had been honed with martial arts. She'd learned the fine art of marksmanship and spent more hours with her guns than some did with lovers. She'd initiated victims' rights groups, supported sober driving advocacy groups, and campaigned for better laws.

Still, they kept drinking, kept driving, kept killing.

Time for that to change.

90 minutes until release

When there had been years left in Sean's sentence, time hadn't weighed as heavily. Time had been more like an endless loop. Get up. Eat. Exercise. Sleep. Repeat. It hadn't grated on his nerves. Today he paced his cell relentlessly, unable to stop.

The seconds dragged and the clocks slowed until he wanted to hurl them at the wardens sneering their disdain.

Freedom was so close but remained out of reach. Unattainable. Still ninety minutes of hell.

90 minutes until release

Nails digging into the wheel, she drove carefully along the freeway.

She hated the freeway. Hated driving.

Every light pole she passed reminded her of Matt and his last moments.

Eighty-seven light poles on the way to work.

Three hundred nineteen to the cemetery.

Each one she passed brought memories and each memory ended with a vision of Matt in death. Another light pole zipped past with every beat of her heart. Heartbeats Matt had missed out on. Heartbeats *that* man was allowed while her boy lay deep in the ground.

Now they were about to let that murderer's heart beat in freedom.

Unacceptable.

Five thousand two hundred and ninety-one.
Ninety-two.

75 minutes until release

So many potential lairs for a long shot. Plenty of hidden shadows and deep corners, but Cam wasn't sure where to choose. Walker had earned a close-up death, one where he would know what was happening even while he remained powerless to stop it.

Being witness to that moment of awareness would be worth the risk of getting in close. Seeing the fear in Walker's eyes and then the knowledge of what was about to happen was a necessity.

Matt hadn't had a chance.

Neither would Walker.

60 minutes until release

Maybe here. Close to the prison gates, but far enough that his equipment wouldn't be jostled by the crowd. The tripod had cost Marty a month's salary. The camera almost half a year's. Worth every penny.

These pictures would capture evil.

So many opportunities for the perfect shot. The bleak background of the prison gates. The thin blue line holding back the angry crowds. Relatives and friends of the victim overcome with emotions.

And Walker himself. His reaction to the protestors and freedom. The juxtaposition of the extreme emotions might be the prize-winning shot.

60 minutes until release

It would be best to stay in the shadows. Walker wouldn't leave the prison without his family's protection. Daddy would provide bodyguards with weapons far superior to any police force and there was no way Jake wanted to be on the receiving end of those.

He was here to get the job done and clean his slate without being recognized. He'd worked too damn hard to be a good lawyer to have this failure on his conscience. Jake might have won the trial, but he'd still been on the losing side.

The changes he'd made since couldn't quite erase the guilt. Working for the prosecutor's office eased some of it, but it also showed him how often the system failed. How hard people worked to keep the guilty free.

Not this time. This time, he'd make up for his mistake. This time, he'd do it right.

60 minutes until release

George saluted one of his buddies as he slid his pickup into a spot a few blocks away from the prison. There was enough time for a couple of brews. Beer cans were lifted in greeting as he crossed the lot and grabbed his own. A man couldn't ask for better friends. Men who shared a dream of making their country what it once was. Too many weasels wriggling their way around the laws.

Once they took their stance today, people would see the right of things. The cowards would crawl back to their shadows and take their lawyers with them.

This would be the kick start their country needed.

60 minutes until release

What would it feel like to kill? To take a life away, to remove a person's future. Would she feel like a god or a demon? She wasn't sure how, but she knew it would change her irrevocably.

She didn't want to be in charge of another's fate. To wipe out his friendships, his loves, his hates. To change the course of history. Would it be easier knowing the death she caused saved other lives? Nita doubted it, but she would soon find out for sure.

60 minutes until release

Impressive as always. Even the tripod was completely unrecognizable and the entire setup took only seventy seconds. More rehearsal could reduce that, but Cam's time was running short.

Better to be a little early than late. Rushing caused mistakes and mistakes were unacceptable. This wasn't the time to screw up a job. Somewhere in the preparations, he'd made a decision. This was it. Time to move on to a new adventure. Time to enjoy the money and explore more of the world.

Sean Walker would have the honor of being Cam's final kill.

45 minutes until release

Like Lady MacBeth, she scrubbed her already clean hands. Even the faintest trace of gasoline needed to be removed if she hoped to escape afterward.

Like the doomed character, Sally didn't believe she was clean or ever would be clean again. If only she could move forward with her life, but with people like Sean Walker out on the streets, she didn't have a choice.

She picked up the soap again.

30 minutes until release

The hidden canister felt heavier than it should. The gaseous contents amounted to almost nothing, but combined with the intentions, the weight became almost unbearable.

Jake didn't want to be a killer, but Matt deserved someone to cross that line for him. An honorable man stepped up for an innocent victim, made sure he got vengeance. A man with principles acknowledged his mistakes and fixed them.

Time to gather his courage and be that man.

15 minutes until release

So much anger. So many people. The crowd was building, far beyond what she had expected. Her nails dug into her palms as she realized she might not be able to get close enough.

Ashley leaned against the light pole and it gave her strength. She would confront Matt's killer with it supporting her.

Five minutes before release

The consequences didn't matter.
Killers should be kept in prison.
Killers.
Sally would soon be one of them. The scent of gasoline would haunt her. She had to remember that consequences didn't matter.

Two minutes before release

The chains thumped against the concrete with each footfall. Only one hundred more times.
Fifty.
Twenty.
Ten.
Sean held his breath for the last five. No more inhaling of fetid prison air. He drew free air into his

lungs.

No more drab. No more dull.

No more restrictions.

The shackles impeded his climb onto the bus, but they would be gone soon. His life lay on the other side of the fence. Once he reached the sidewalk, he'd be truly free.

Release

Towering walls of barbed wire protected the innocent from the inmates. But these ashen barricades were opening up to spew one of the corrupt out into the world. One who had taken a life and was moving on to live his without any further penalty.

The crisscrossing wires blurred the view, but Cam was able to see the small bus pull away from the building toward the waiting crowds.

Toward the end.

Release

Her pulse raced and her fingers trembled on the gun hidden in her pocket. She had to control herself. The bus inched toward the barbed wire. The gate eased open, the bus crept through, and Nita thought of her Matt as she blinked back the tears.

Release

Through the dingy windows of the bus, Marty saw the guards stand and then approach Walker. They didn't speak as they unlocked the handcuffs and the shackles.

The chains dropped and he shook out his hands, rubbed his wrists. He moved toward the exit, didn't spare a single glance to the gathered crowds.

Walker took five steps and reached the top of the stairs before he paused, then went down the steps.

Release

The shot was lined up.
No obstacles.
No hesitation.
Time.

Release

Sally had to be closer. None of it worked unless she was close enough to use the gasoline and then the matches. She hadn't expected so many officers. Most prisoners were released with little fanfare and no crowds.

Rich and cocky, Sean Walker's trial had drawn more attention than most, making her job more difficult. And while he was walking away early, his freedom wasn't going to last long.

As long as she could get closer.

Release

The protesters didn't matter. The cameras didn't matter. Even his family didn't matter. All that mattered was the air.

Fresh air. Free air.
Breathe in, breathe out.
Free.

One minute after release

Straightening from her light pole, she watched Walker step down from the bus. She hadn't been able to get close enough to do what she'd come to do. Taking a deep breath, Ashley raised her voice and yelled words she'd never uttered before. Vile, reprehensible words. Words meant to impact. Words meant to harm.

Words no one heard in the surrounding chaos.

One minute after release

The first rock missed its target and banged off the bus, bouncing into the gutter. George aimed the next carefully.

One minute after release

She wanted emotional and physical damage before death took him. He would smell the gasoline first and know exactly what was coming next. He wouldn't be able to stop it.

The noise and confusion should make it easy to be close enough to toss the matches before Sally blended into the crowd.

One minute after release

Nita gripped her grandmother's derringer. The dainty pistol had taken down more than one burglar in its day. Today, it would take down a killer.

She knew it would cost her almost as much, but her freedom was a small price to pay. Her Matt would be able to rest in peace.

Soon.

Once the bus drove away. Once the view was clear.

One minute after release

The trigger felt cool and comfortable.

No one could see; the cover was perfect. The setup

was better.

Camera. Rifle.

Two shots for the price of one.

One minute after release

Free air.

In. Out.

Free—

90 seconds after release

Cam missed that perfect moment. Not enough time to trade the trigger for the shutter.

The wide eyes, the rounded mouth. Shock. Confusion. Fear.

Perfect.

But the camera captured the second moment. Glassy eyes, the first hints of blood leaking from the wound.

Unable to resist the opportunity, he clicked the shutter again and again.

Memories.

Too good to pass up.

Two minutes after release

Walker was shot no more than a few yards away from where Jake watched while someone else avenged Matt.

The bodyguards would soon be searching the crowd for suspicious and familiar faces. He couldn't risk sticking around. Couldn't risk being caught with his own weapon because Walker's men wouldn't be asking questions or checking forensics.

No, they'd kill quickly and without compunction. He'd put himself at risk for nothing. Not only had he not taken care of Walker, but he'd gotten close to the front where he could be spotted.

Glad for the chaos, Jake kept his eyes down and backed away.

Two minutes after release

She flinched at the blood oozing from the hole in Walker's forehead. Her feet stumbled and she knocked into the person behind her then kept moving.

Death had been quick.

Not what she'd wanted. Or planned.

He'd needed to suffer. Her parents had suffered for hours. He was gone in moments.

It wasn't fair.

He should be burning, swatting uselessly at the flames as they slowly peeled off his skin and left him screaming in agony.

He hadn't earned an easy death. None of them had. The next one would pay.

Two minutes after release

George grinned and raised a fist in victory as the body dropped to the ground. Even better than his own plan.

He hoped the shooter was already on the move. He hoped they'd get away and keep doing the good work.

Time for another beer.

Two minutes after release

Someone else had shot Walker. Someone had taken her shot away from her. Walker had killed her Matt, her lover, her future.

It should have been her shot.

Two minutes after release

He'd spent too much time. The artist's ego had superseded common sense. Cam forced himself to move steadily as he untwisted the rifle barrel and secured it back into the tripod.

Disassembling the rest of the gun took only seconds, then another thirty to conceal the parts about his person.

Time to blend in.

Two minutes after release

Blood splattered her blouse in a shade to match the polish on her nails. More of it dripped down the face of her son's killer.

Her hand dropped to her side and her journal slipped to the ground. It hit at the same moment as the killer's crumpled body. He would never read the words, never know what he'd done to her son. To her. To his fiancee. To his friends.

He would never know.

She watched the blood seep and spread. Watched his life drain away.

Her heart ached. It ached for them all.

The End

Jemi Fraser lives in beautiful Northern Ontario where she works hard and plays harder with both her family and her students. Holding an ever-present mug of Chai tea, she spends her free time baking cookies and writing Happy Ever Afters. The world can always use more of both.
www.jemifraser.blogspot.ca

UNTIL RELEASE

www.twitter.com/jemifraser
www.facebook.com/profile.
php?id=100013354501204

**A Writer's Digest 101 Best Websites for Writers
and The Write Life's 100 Best Websites for
Writers**

The Insecure Writer's Support Group was founded by science fiction author Alex J. Cavanaugh in September, 2011. Its purpose - to encourage, support, and inform. The website is a database resource for writers and authors, with weekly guests and tips, thousands of links, and a monthly newsletter. There is also a monthly bloghop the first Wednesday of every month, a Facebook and Instagram group, and @TheIWSG on Twitter.

Website: www.insecurewriterssupportgroup.com
Facebook: www.facebook.com/groups/IWSG13
Twitter: www.twitter.com/TheIWSG
Instagram: www.instagram.com/theiwsg
Email: admin@insecurewriterssupportgroup.com
Newsletter signup:
http://insecurewriterssupportgroup.us12.list-manage.com/subscribe?u=b058c62fa7ffb4280355e8854&id=cc6abce571

CPSIA information can be obtained
at www.ICGtesting.com
Printed in the USA
FSHW04n1413190418
47038FS

9 781939 844545